In Those Days

The Gregg Press Western Fiction Series
Priscilla Oaks, Editor

In Those Days
Harvey Fergusson

with a new introduction by
William T. Pilkington

Gregg Press
A division of G. K. Hall & Co., Boston, 1978

This is a complete photographic reprint of a work first published in New York by Alfred A. Knopf in 1929.

Text copyright 1929 by Alfred A. Knopf, Inc.
Reprinted by arrangement with Francis Fergusson.
Introduction copyright © 1978 by William T. Pilkington.

Grateful acknowledgement is made to Saul Cohen for generously providing a rare early copy of *In Those Days: An Impression of Change* for reproduction in this Gregg Press edition.

Frontmatter designed by Designworks, Inc. of Cambridge, Massachusetts.

Printed on permanent/durable acid-free paper and bound in the United States of America.

Republished in 1978 by Gregg Press, A Division of G. K. Hall & Co., 70 Lincoln Street, Boston, Massachusetts 02111.

First Printing, October 1978

Library of Congress Cataloging in Publication Data

Fergusson, Harvey, 1890–1971.
   In those days.

   (The Gregg Press western fiction series)
   Reprint of the ed. published by Knopf, New York.
   I. Title. II. Series.
PZ3.F388In 1978 [PS3511.E55] 813'.5'2 78-13366
ISBN 0-8398-2472-6

Introduction

Harvey Fergusson's roots were deeply embedded in the red earth of New Mexico. Born in 1890 in Albuquerque, he was descended from families who were important in his state's politics and commerce. His father, Harvey Butler Fergusson, was territorial representative and later the first Congressman from New Mexico, when the territory became a state. His maternal grandfather, Franz Huning, was owner and operator of one of Albuquerque's first mercantile stores. Fergusson himself loved the mountains and desert of northern New Mexico and, as a young man, roamed across hundreds of square miles of what was then still virtually unexplored wilderness. All his life he read avidly and widely in the history of New Mexico and of the American West. And yet in 1912, at the age of 22, he moved away from New Mexico and never again made his official residence in that state.

In the ensuing decades Fergusson lived for extended periods in such places as Washington, D. C., New York City, Los Angeles, and Berkeley, California. At various times in his life he earned an ample, though hardly luxurious, income by doing political reportage for a number of East Coast and Middlewestern newspapers, grinding out formula stories for mass-circulation periodicals, and working as a screenwriter for several Hollywood motion picture companies. Fergusson's claim to serious critical attention as a writer, however, rests on 14 full-length works (ten of which are novels), published between the years 1921 and 1954. Almost all these books are set in or are about New Mexico. Clearly the New Mexican landscape and history inhabited his adult imagination with vivid urgency, even as he lived most of his life far from the borders of his native state.

Fergusson has been the most curiously neglected of important 20th-century writers from the American West. Even within the region he is not particularly well-known—perhaps because, as a young man, he chose to live in the large cities of the East rather than in the great open spaces of his home country. Other Western writers—Walter Van Tilburg Clark, Vardis Fisher, A. B. Guthrie, Wallace Stegner, Frederick Manfred—have reputations as serious regional artists that seem to outweigh Fergusson's modest renown. I do not hesitate to assert, however, that Fergusson's achievement is easily the equal of that of any of his more celebrated colleagues. The best of his novels—*The Blood of the Conquerors* (1921), *Wolf Song* (1927), *In Those Days* (1929), *Grant of Kingdom* (1950), and *The Conquest of Don Pedro* (1954)—comprise as distinguished a body of fiction as any yet fashioned by a Western American writer.

When he died in Berkeley in 1971, Fergusson had lived to enjoy at least a modicum of long-delayed recognition and acclaim. During the last couple of decades of his life, several writers and collectors of Western literature "discovered" his books and attempted to call more general attention to them. Saul Cohen, Lawrence Clark Powell, and John R. Milton deserve special mention for their pioneering efforts in this regard. Critics have begun in recent years to examine the works in detail in order to isolate their special virtues. Cecil Robinson, for instance, in his highly regarded *With the Ears of Strangers: The Mexican in American Literature* (Tucson: University of Arizona Press, 1963), comments lengthily and admiringly on a half-dozen of Fergusson's best regional books. James K. Folsom's pamphlet, *Harvey Fergusson* (Austin, Texas: Steck-Vaughn, 1969), supplies a useful introductory essay on the writer's philosophy and fictional concerns. William T. Pilkington's *Harvey Fergusson* (Boston: Twayne Publishers, 1975) is the first book-length biographical-critical study of the author, and includes full analyses of each of the works. As favorable critical responses accumulate, acknowledgement of Fergusson's accomplishment grows. Hopefully the writer's posthumous reputation will acquire, in the not-too-distant future, dimensions more commensurate with his actual, very considerable achievement.

In Those Days: An Impression of Change, the author's sixth novel, was published in 1929. The story is loosely based on the life and career of Fergusson's grandfather, Franz Huning. When he died around the turn of the century, Huning left a memoir which his grandson read for the first time in the 1920s. (The memoir, under the title *Trader on the Santa Fe Trail,* was published, with notes by Fergusson's sister Lina Fergusson Browne, in 1973.) By his own account Huning was born in Germany, came to America as a teenager in 1848, got a job driving oxen on freight caravans on the Santa Fe Trail, and first saw Santa Fe, at the terminal of the long trail, on Christmas Day, 1850. From that day to the end of his life he remained a New Mexican.

The young Huning was involved in several adventurous escapades appropriate to the wild Western setting in which he found himself. He once trekked into Apache country to buy cheap mules that the Indians had stolen in Mexico; he and his party, however, were trapped in a snowstorm in the White Mountains of what is now Arizona, and were lucky to escape with their lives. After this incident he settled down to a position as secretary and interpreter for a priest; he later held a similar position with a federal judge. In the late 1850s he opened a general store on the plaza in Albuquerque, an enterprise that was an immediate success. Over the years he also built a flour mill and sawmill and bought a great deal of farm and ranch land around Albuquerque.

In the 1880s Huning constructed in Albuquerque an enormous house modeled after a German castle on the Rhine; indeed the structure came to be popularly known as "Castle Huning." At about this point in his career he had a chance to become a true financial giant, a millionaire, an opportunity he consciously passed up. In his old age, when his grandson knew him, Huning's possessions had dwindled to his beloved castle and the grounds on which it stood. According to Fergusson, his grandfather was not really a businessman. In fact, he disliked and distrusted the kind of urban businessmen that the railroads brought to town in the late nineteenth century.

Franz Huning was a merchant-adventurer, a creature of the old Southwest who was, as he himself realized, wholly alien to the bustling commercial atmosphere of turn-of-the-century Albuquerque.

The reader will recognize, of course, many parallels between the career of Franz Huning and that of Robert Jayson, the central character of *In Those Days*. In the novel Fergusson subtly points up the historical importance (an idea he develops further in *The Conquest of Don Pedro*) of the Western merchants and storekeepers. Their role in the "taming" of the West was, as a matter of fact, probably more significant than that of the violent types so widely portrayed in popular fiction and films. In the Southwest the storekeeper was often the most powerful person in his community. As the town's chief supplier and creditor, he possessed considerable political leverage, the delicate exercise of which became a kind of local art form.

The principal purpose of *In Those Days*, however, is not to provide the reader with a mercantile history of the Southwest; it is rather to illustrate dramatically one of the author's favorite themes. The novel's subtitle, *An Impression of Change*, provides a clue to that theme. Fergusson believed that the history of the West was a great drama of endless change and of people's responses to change—their meeting or failing to meet the challenge of change. When an individual resists the swift current of change, the author theorized, that individual and the institutions of which he is a part become rigid and inflexible; they are no longer viable. Concerning *In Those Days*, Fergusson once commented that his aim in writing the book was to trace "the long curve of a human destiny"—to take an overview from which the forces that shaped that destiny might be more clearly discerned. The more chronologically detached our view, the author claimed, the better we see that Jayson, the novel's protagonist, was "dominated rather than dominating. Time and Change are the mighty characters in this story."

In order to follow "the long curve of a human destiny," Fergusson begins his tale with a portrait of Robert Jayson as a callow but energetic youth, lured by the "westering" impulse from his Connecticut home to territorial New Mexico.

Introduction

He concludes the story by showing us Jayson as an impoverished "old-timer," a man content to relax and daydream about the glorious excitement of the past. Jayson's life is long and eventful—a life which stretches, in terms of regional history, from the freight wagon to the automobile. But it is this very circumstance, I think, that gives rise to one of the book's most serious flaws. The novel is not really lengthy enough to project a sense of fullness in chronicling so long a life. Fergusson settles, therefore, for zeroing in on four crucial stages of Jayson's career. Inevitably such a technique, and the abrupt shifts and lapses in chronology that it requires, makes the narrative seem choppy and disjointed in places. The reader wishes for more detail and smoother transitions than the brevity of the story can possibly allow.

Despite weaknesses, *In Those Days* is one of Fergusson's most interesting and readable novels. The author's implicit sympathy and understanding for his main character (a sympathy and understanding no doubt derived from his emotional response to the fate of his grandfather) make the work one of his gentlest and wisest books. Jayson lives an active and in many ways successful life. He swims in the current of change as long as his health and supply of energy hold out. Eventually, when old age robs him of his will to struggle, he thickens into immobility, slipping into that stasis—that phase of life when "catastrophes and triumphs look for the moment just alike" (p. 266) and the future is "a matter of the utmost unconcern" (p. 266)—that is in effect spiritual death. This is the "curve" of Jayson's destiny; it is also the curve of destiny that, to one degree or another, the lives of most people follow. Robert Jayson is not one of the great and memorable heroes of Western fiction. But in his quiet way, he provides—in his useful and productive career and in his graceful old age—a rather striking model of how to conduct an honorable and courageous life in the midst of those implacable forces of Time and Change.

William T. Pilkington
Tarleton State University
Stephenville, Texas

ix

IN THOSE DAYS

CONTENTS

FIRST PART
WAGONS

Chapter One

I N those days, soon after the Civil War, thousands of wagons, stage coaches, buckboards, ambulances and even one-horse carts and buggies went rolling West.

What had started as a few traders taking a long chance, going without a road or a map to find a market a thousand miles away, became in thirty years a commerce worth its millions and a migration that left towns half-deserted in its wake.

Freight moved in great wagons with five-foot wheels and high white covers. Four thousand pounds was a wagon load and it took twelve or sixteen mules to haul one. Grand pianos and sawmills went west in wagons and glass and silk were shipped insured and perfect. One company of freighters had four thousand wagons on the road and used twenty thousand oxen, ten thousand mules and horses and five thousand men.

Freighters used to load their wagons high and top-heavy so they would rock and sway along the road, shifting the weight from side to side, speeding them on the level. Sometimes on hillsides it took twelve men with ropes to hold a great staggering wagon to the road and sometimes on steep grades the brakes burned out and mules were crushed and mangled by two-tons wagons. The quicksands of western rivers swallowed wagons whole and they bogged and stuck for days in the prairie mud. But when the going was good and the whips cracked and sixteen mules hit the collar, great wagons went dancing west like big-hipped happy girls. They moved in lines miles long and sometimes, on open prairie, in parallel columns across a front half a mile wide. At night they curled up and rested in circles of fire.

Besides all these freight trains, thousands of immigrants went west every year, looking for land and gold, littering the prairie with dead stock and broken wheels. They used everything that would hold a load from hand-carts to conestoga wagons and carried everything that belongs to a family, including chickens, milk cows, cats, goats and canary birds. Babies were born in wagons and people died in them and were buried beside the road for coyotes to dig up. Men would stop in the middle of the prairie to get married or have a fight or sing a hymn . . .

Past the slow-moving wagons both ways went the tall blue Concord coaches of the stage lines with six mules in a fast trot or sometimes in a gallop. First there were monthly stages and then weekly and then daily, going twenty to forty miles between stations, changing mules in three minutes,

[4]

never stopping longer day or night. They made a hundred miles a day and you could go from St. Louis to San Francisco in twenty-six days if you had the fare and could stand the shaking. Nine passengers rode inside a coach and a driver and two guards outside. The guards were armed with Colt's new patent revolving rifles and pistols, the deadliest weapons the world had ever seen. And they needed them. Indians seldom bothered a wagon train but Comanchee, Arapahoe, Cheyenne and Sioux all struck at the stage lines in those days when wheels were cutting the buffalo range to pieces. . . . Anxious guards would see bobbing heads of horsemen over hilltops. Suddenly they would wheel and come—brown naked yelling men lashing ponies, dropping behind their mounts as they drew closer, shooting under stretched necks of running horses. Then drivers whipped and swore, women screamed and guards lying flat on rocking stage-tops pumped smoke and flame. Sometimes shot horses plunged and fell and wild men swarmed over a coach and wiped it out in blood and ashes. But another coach came next day . . .

In those days any man not securely anchored by woman or property was likely to ride a coach or a wagon West. It was in the air to go West. Newspapers and gossip were full of the West. Men came back from the West to tell lies no stranger than the truth. Everybody knew some-body who had gone West. Guide books to the Wild West were best sellers . . .

Men who had killed and stolen went West if they got away. Men who had failed went West with their assets and left their liabilities behind. Men of imagination were struck by an idea of the West as by disease. Western fever was as real as smallpox and sent men chasing dreams across a continent. The sting of a woman's no sent many a man West and many another went to lose a woman he couldn't stand. Men on the verge of suicide went West instead of pulling a trigger or jumping off a bridge. Unwanted sons of the rich were sent West on remittance and unwanted sons of the poor were started West on a fence rail or at the point of a gun.

Life-sick youth went inevitably West in search of a better world and found that what it fled was before as well as behind. . . .

Having a West made Americans different from men who lived in small and known worlds. . . . West was the way out of everything. West was the home of hope.

Chapter Two

MANY A NIGHT Robert Jayson lay between wagon wheels, wrapped in scanty blankets, listening to wind in the grass or to the cold steady voice of spring rain and thinking miserably.

Often he lay thinking until wheel spokes barred a paling dawn sky.

Much of this time he thought about his sweetheart Elizabeth. He nearly always remembered her as he had seen her last, standing on the front steps waving him good-by. She had on her best blue silk dress. It was a voluminous dress outflouncing over many stiff petticoats from a short bodice, so that she looked like a great blue flower upside down. Sun shone on her pale silky hair and on a disregarded tear that he could see like dew on grass from way down the road.

That tear shed for his going seemed to follow and sting him and call him a fool. For she had not wanted him to go. She did not doubt that he would make money and come back but she would rather have had him stay home and be poor. And when he lay listening to rain in the night he sickened with a conviction that she had been the wiser.

It seemed as though just before he left he had

[7]

learned more of Elizabeth than in all the rest of the year they had kept company. She had always been a sweet mystery to him, protected by his own shyness, wrapped in reticence and in yards and yards of skirt. He had known no more about the real state of her mind than he did about the shape of her legs. They had kissed only timidly and a few times until that last night when she surprised him with the claiming strength of her arms, the hot wet pressure of her mouth. And what made him squirm now was the recollection that he had ended that moment. He had put her gently away, not knowing why. Her flaming face and bitten lip blamed him still but not half as much as he blamed himself. Listening to rain in the night he felt as though he would give all the gold on Pike's Peak to have her kiss him that way again.

She had played her harp and sung for him that last night. . . . Annie Laurie and that other one she liked about my false lover stole my rose but Oh . . . She had prayed for him and cried a little because he wouldn't kneel beside her. In a serious logical way he had decided against the possibility of a responsive Providence and he stuck to his conviction. He stuck to his plan, too, although her tears and music made him feel soft and helpless.

He had stuck to his plan and here he was. Why had he come? He knew he had dreamed of making much money which he could not hope to do at home. He knew that faraway places had always called him. He knew too that he was dissatisfied with himself and hoped to be a different man in a different world.

He could review his reasons, but he could not recover a spark of the mood that had moved him. He felt sometimes like starting back on foot.

Homesick and in love he took little notice of what he saw because what he remembered was so much more vivid.

At first they toiled through a rainy country just turning green. He was wet and cold most of the time and grew sick of the crack of whips, the shouts and curses, the suck and splutter of heavy teams in mud. Warmer days brought a swarm of mosquitoes that kept him awake all one night and made him puff a pipe till his tongue burned.

The Arkansas was so high when they crossed it that wagons floated and mules swam in the middle, and his vitals curled up inside of him at sight of the swift red growling water. He was afraid of things like that and loathed his own fear, longed to conquer it.

In the sandhills beyond, spring sun had brought out rattlesnakes by the dozen. Crawling writhing black and yellow, hideously beautiful, coiled in mottled buzzing masses, they filled him with unreasonable horror. Teamsters made a sport of snapping off their heads with dexterous deadly whiplashes, turning up their livid squirming bellies to the sun.

Beyond the river, the country was barren and vacant as the sea and made him long for a little green valley where a wooded hill cuddled an upland pasture and a white house showed through trees. . . . This country seemed no more made for human habitation than the moon.

He saw buffalo and antelope at first in moving distant masses and flashing pale figures of speed, and then he saw a beautiful band of antelope run close and men shouted and shot with any kind of a gun. Some of the swift gray figures fell kicking and bleeding and some, wounded, limped and dragged away. He saw the dead hung up, throats cut to give purple spurts of blood and bellies ripped open to let steaming masses of entrails fall on the ground and he could not eat the meat any more than he could have torn and eaten a living thing.

Everything surprised and disgusted him. He was surprised and disgusted to find what an inadequate being he was in a strange world.

Farther West the country was powdery gritty dry. Wheel and hoof raised clouds of dust that choked men and mules and laid its color on everything. When a high wind blew it seemed to lift and carry the land, so thick was the air with flying sand that filled the eyes and stung like shot. At its worst mules refused to face it and teams fell into a milling confusion. At every stop teamsters raised a sharp tattoo hammering tires back onto wheels that had swollen in the wet and now shrank in the drought.

Sometimes he sat beside a driver on a hard seat and sometimes he toiled on foot with a bent head beside a laboring mule. It seemed to him he dragged a load of memory and regret as heavy as a wagon. It was pain to look back and despair to look forward and the moment was a travail to endure.

It struck him as a revelation that life was a thing of toil and blood and he had never before tasted either.

He despised himself for a weakling but he did not pity himself and he knew he would never go back now until he had made money.

Never had days seemed so much alike or so long. He was amazed as weeks went by how remote remembered things became—the shining hair of his beloved, the old white house and the green valley. It seemed incredible that he had ever kissed Elizabeth or sat down before his aunt's white breakfast table to put thick cream in coffee and spread strawberry jam on hot muffins.

Surely he had been toiling for years across this

dusty desert and would toil on eternally, for it was endless.

Yet even while he loathed it he was getting used to it all—to walking and to hard rocking wagon seats and to the ground for a bed. He lay awake no longer but slept dreamless. To be dirty and sunburnt, to have cracked lips tortured by alkali dust, came to seem the common human lot. Tired of beans and hard bread he ate wild meat and found it good.

His blistered aching feet became calloused and his nerves seemed to thicken as his skin did. The shouts and curses, the creak and rattle had racked him at first and now he noticed them only when they ceased.

He lay on the earth by night and by day the earth rose in dust and covered him.

Lulled by toil and monotony he thought and dreamed less and less. Wagons and dust and the hard earth were immediate and everything else was faint and faraway.

Everything he knew and loved was fading out of his life—everything that had made him what he was. He felt lost and incomplete.

The unconquered country about him was hardly a home for men but only what might become one. And he, trudging westward alone, was hardly a person any more, but only a bit of dust and blood following the sun.

Chapter Three

ABEL DOXEY had a store in a little adobe town beside the Rio Grande south of Santa Fe.

The valley there was flat and rich, green with crops and spotted with silver waters. On either side of it were sandy flats where water crawled far underground, dead mesas of purple lava and little spiney mountain ranges with dry canyons and sharp-cut rimrocks.

In the valley a man could live safe, but on either side of it and North and South the Navajos, Apaches and Comanchees owned the earth and menaced every intruder.

This town was more than a hundred years old and the Mexicans that built it got their grants from the King of Spain. When Mexico cut loose from the King it made little difference to these people, so far away. When the Americans read another proclamation, ran up yet another flag, and planted a few Yankee judges here and there, it made little more. Soldiers came and stayed a few years and went away again, leaving a tall white flag pole in the plaza, a scattering of blue-eyed babies, a store run by a gringo and a poker game in the back room of a saloon.

More wagons from Missouri came every year and that made some difference. The gringo colony grew from three to nine, the poor people began to wear store clothes and the Ricos began melting down their hammered silver to buy red plush furniture, gilt-framed mirrors, velvet and broadcloth. . . . But still as before a few rich Mexicans owned the country and ruled it with the help of the church, raised grain and fruit in the valley and a million scrubby sheep on the hills. They no longer bought and sold slaves but one could still own a man by giving him credit and rent a girl from her mother if she was poor. Forms and appearances changed a little but the good old ways were stubborn.

The town was built around a plaza, wide and treeless, with a depression in the middle that held water half the year, breeding mosquitoes and a summer chorus of small green frogs. On one side of it the old adobe church lifted twin towers twice as high as anything else in town and rang an old sweet Spanish bell for early mass and vespers. The dwelling of the padre stood next door with apple trees behind it and hollyhocks in front. It looked across at the long low pillared portale of Don Aragon's great house, whitewashed and iron-barred, reaching amply back through two placitas to an adobe-walled corral, orchards and fields of grain.

These monuments to church and aristocracy,

both nearly a century old, gave the town design, dignity and a look of permanence.

Abel Doxey's store, which filled another whole side of the town square, had been there only twenty years but it covered as much space as the Aragon house and it drew a greater crowd than the church. It too had a long front porch, decorated with bright new blue and red wagons and shining plows chained to iron rings in the floor. Within, it was an impressive concentration of all the goods men live by. It was piled and cluttered with boxes, sacks, barrels and bolts and festooned with saddlery and harness. Counters were bright with knives, pots and pans, dishes and trinkets, and rifles, muskets and shotguns armed its walls. It had a drug counter and a liquor counter and its air was heavy with the smell of whisky, new leather, raw wool, onions, coffee and tobacco. Most of the day it was filled with slow voices of barter and with the clink of silver and the rattle and thud of moving merchandise. A wide yard was formed behind it by two rows of storerooms and a ten foot wall with a great double iron-bound gate. Almost daily wagons rattled dustily in and noisy Mexicans unloaded them, shouting each other abundant directions and grunting under heavy backloads.

The Aragon place and the church hadn't changed in fifty years but Doxey was always building something or putting in a new line. . . .

The rest of the settlement clustered around this triumvirate and straggled up and down the valley. Little brown houses with blue doors and windows sat under cottonwood trees. Each had a bit of orchard, patchy fields of grain, clover and chile, and a long stretch of wet alkaline pasture reaching to the cottonwood bosky by the river. Redwing blackbirds and meadow larks were many and vocal and almost every cottonwood tree contained the soft voice of a dove.

In Doxey's store Robert began his life as a pioneer, sitting on a high stool in a small room making a fine pattern of neat penmanship on pages of a ledger. . . . Was it for this he had come so far? . . . When not busy on the books he studied Spanish by translating Don Quixote with the aid of a grammar and dictionary. He read Don Quixote because it was the only Spanish book he had. He found it hard to understand, ridiculous and often shocking.

Doxey told him to get out in the store and try to wait on people when he had time. That was the only way he would ever learn the language. But he shrank from trying. Whenever Doxey poked his head through the office door Robert was busy on the books.

He was a good bookkeeper, and in the books he read the story of the store. He saw profits were enormous and almost all who lived in the town, and many from miles away, were in debt to Doxey. He saw how the store reached out and gathered in all the wool and grain, the hides and pelts and laid a lien on land and sheep and cattle.

This was more than a store, it was a power. It held men by catering to their needs, it dazzled them with gimcracks and seduced them with luxuries. Mexican wagons came from fifty miles away, tall-hatted men riding on the seats, black-shawled women bouncing on the load, to trade all they had raised and mortgage all they hoped for, buying what they needed first, then all that took their eyes until Doxey would give them no more credit.

Every evening when he was done work Robert walked around the corner of the store to his supper at Tolliver's hotel, which was only another sprawling house of mud with a long dining room on one side of its front hall and a saloon and gambling joint on the other. Sometimes fifteen or twenty sat down to eat and sometimes only five or six, but always most of the conversation was Mexican and most of the food was beef and beans swimming in red chile.

Beef was in big chunks with bones in them. Diners tossed these over their shoulders and Tolliver's dogs caught them on the fly and crunched them with a noise that offended refined young Robert. He sat trying to fish out pieces of meat

[17]

not too hot for his tongue, thinking of fried chicken, apple pie and Elizabeth, wishing he had never come West to grow up with the country. . . . He wished Horace Greeley might be sentenced to eat chile con carne twice a day for two weeks. . . . He wished Judge Turnbull wouldn't drink coffee out of a saucer with a noise like a heavy shower on a shingle roof.

After supper Robert went out and sat on a bench in front of the store and smoked his pipe. Mosquitoes came tinily singing about his ears and little bats did zig-zags in a deepening sky. Almost all the men in town sat down somewhere along the plaza in the evening, and almost all the women did a slow promenade in couples and threes. They all wore shapeless dresses of cotton print and great black shawls which they managed with a certain skill and grace. In the day their shawls were always hooded against the sun but in the evening they showed their faces. Most of them were swarthy, many were pock-marked and dirty but there were a few clean pretty girls. Their eyes and skins were soft. They had soft voices and lazy movements. They seemed to be made of a softer stuff than women he had known. They chattered with each other and looked back over their shoulders and laughed and ogled at men.

Robert felt a little better every time a pretty girl went by, although none of them, he knew, could ever mean anything to him. He was shy of women even when he spoke their language.

When it grew dark and the sky swallowed the mountains, the plaza slowly emptied except for a few low-talking voices, the flare of a match, a hidden laugh. Robert rose and walked alone in dark roads, filled with a large heavy gloom of general loneliness and a small sharp ache of desire that made him think of the one hot kiss of Elizabeth as the one great lost opportunity of his life.

It became frightfully quiet, as though all the ancient silence of surrounding deserts had poured down on the little town with the dark and buried it deep. Only voices of dogs broke this heavy stillness, dog answering dog farther and farther away, until doleful fainting dog voices were lost in distance.

When he could stand it outside no longer Robert went to his room and lit a candle.

One night he had slept at Tolliver's and waked up burning with the bites of bedbugs. Next day at Doxey's suggestion he had rented this room from an old Mexican woman. Doxey said it was clean and it seemed to be, with shining white walls, a white bed, a homemade chair and table and a hard dirt floor partly covered with a native woolen carpet, checkered black and gray. It had one window with a double wooden shutter but no glass. With its white, thick sound-proof walls it was like a tomb inside. Here Robert wrote long careful letters and then sat thinking sadly of love, death and the improbability of Divine Providence.

No man could keep this up for long. After a few solitary evenings he began going back to Tolliver's and sitting in a corner of the bar. He felt he had no business there, for he neither drank nor gambled, but he had come to realize that in the evening a man has to go where people are if only to hear voices.

Sometimes few were in the barroom and sometimes teamsters and Mexicans filled it with loud talk and scrape of muddy boots and smell of whisky traveling from bottle to belly. When he had a crowd Tolliver banked a game they called *Chusa* and almost the whole room gathered around his table to bet which hole a little ivory ball would pick to stop in. Tolliver, tall, lean and narrow, walrus-whiskered and unsmiling, never raised his eyes from the game. It was gossip he insured his winnings with a skillful knee against a table leg.

On quieter evenings there was only a private poker game, with young Diego Aragon and Tom Foote from the store invariably sitting. Sometimes Judge Turnbull took a hand and more rarely old man Skillman, who was now postmaster but lived in a past of beaver-trapping and Indian fights. Often several others played but these four were Tolliver's steady customers who came every evening. They all acknowledged Robert's existence with a nod and Tom Foote invited him to drink and took it calmly when he refused. He wished afterwards he had accepted. He had to do something others did.

Young Aragon, aristocrat, with his fifty-dollar hat and his twenty-dollar boots, his silver spurs and Spanish profile, paid Robert least heed and annoyed him most. This young Mexican, heir apparent to more land than he would ever see, drank and gambled, loafed around the plaza staring at girls, rode furiously a black lathering stallion, and did all this with an air of high-nosed all-spurning pride. He contrived to seem superior without doing a thing to prove that he was. Robert was a man of little malice but he felt a recurrent desire to see young Aragon take some kind of tumble.

Judge Turnbull, who was the law for a judicial district of enormous size, inhabited mostly by jackrabbits, who had driven all the way from Kentucky behind his own trotting horse, was courtly-cordial to the newcomer the first time his aqueous, nearsighted gaze happened to focus on Robert.

He gave greeting, came over and sat down, bulging heavily forward in a stiff shirt front brightly decorated with saffron of soft-boiled egg. It was said he always ordered three eggs, two to eat and one for his shirt front, which was immaculate only on alternate Sundays. His cuffs he changed less

often for he kept record on them of legal pro-
ceedings and was sometimes seen to refer to his
linen concerning matters three weeks old. His face
was a deep sclerotic red under a wide black hat and
he exhaled perfume of the private Kentucky stock
which he began drinking daily before breakfast.

The judge inquired of Robert where he came from
and what he did, congratulated him on his valuable
connections, assured him the country contained a
great future for a young man, and spoke at some
length, oratorically, on the fructifications and ex-
pansions that would follow the advent of the At-
lantic and Pacific railroad. Those who denied that
a railroad could be laid across the desert were
either perfidious liars or abysmal fools. . . . Every
noun in the judge's vocabulary was preceded by
one to three sonorous adjectives and his voice
filled the room and absorbed the ears of all, making Robert feel painfully conspicuous.

Having finished with the railroad, he remembered Robert was there and asked him what he
was doing toward learning Spanish. Robert replied he was reading Don Quixote in the origi-
nal. This brought from the Judge's broad and
mobile nostrils a snort of amusement.

"You'll never learn it that way, m'boy," he
bellowed, "You'll have to get you a nice little
sleeping dictionary. . . . That's the way we all
do out here!" He gave Robert a friendly stab be-

tween the ribs with a large hairy finger and his bulbous stomach shook out a deep chuckle, while all smiled and Robert blushed and was glad to see the Judge withdraw.

One by one they all took notice of the shy, misplaced-looking stranger who sat silent in a corner, obviously neither belonging there nor having any where else to go.

Tolliver's little girl came and stood in front of him with a finger in her mouth and her head on one side. She was a precocious, impertinent pretty child of ten with the brown eyes and black hair of a Mexican mother, already showing the restless uncertainty that goes with mixed blood in a country where different breeds meet and mingle.

Robert smiled at her uncomfortably and she tossed her head and turned away with quick childish contempt. Tom Foote caught her and sat her on his knee as he always did when he had a chance. "You're my girl, ain't you Grace? When you grow up a little more we're gonna get married, ain't we?" he bantered, and Grace squirmed and nodded and held her place until her mother, a big-bosomed slatternly voluptuous woman, came and dragged her squalling out of the room.

Old Skillman gave Robert a shy nod and a keen look every morning for a week without ever saying a word. He still wore his hair long, after the fashion of mountain men, and it was nearly white.

He had the quick restless eye of a hunter and the dignity of an old man still supple straight and lean. Robert had a fellow-feeling for him because he seemed to stand apart and lonely. He drank nothing until Saturday night, and then he squared up to the bar, laid down a dollar and took drink after drink slowly and morosely, staring a long time at each little red glass before he downed it with a quick toss of his head. The poker players glanced at him nervously and Tolliver took the bottle away and went out of the room, but Skillman hammered on the bar with another dollar and brought back Tolliver and the bottle without saying a word. When he had taken five or six drinks he turned his back on the bar, leaned against it, folded his arms and surveyed the room, his blue eyes glinting under white brows in a flushed and weathered face with a look of troubled eagerness. His eyes showed something inside him burning its way out like coals in a banked fire. They discovered Robert and immediately he came over and sat down beside him. . . .

"Listen, yo're a stranger, ain't you?" he said in a low voice. "Well, listen . . . come over here. . . ." Firmly he led Robert farther away from the others and sat down beside him again. With a hand on his knee, leaning toward him, breathing whisky in his face, he began to tell a story. It was a muddled wandering story all about something that happened thirty years ago when Skillman was a trapper. Out of a heap of smothering detail Robert fished the fact that thirty years ago Skillman had married a Mexican girl in a little town way down the valley, had lived with her a while and gone away on a trapping trip to the headwaters of the Gila. Of the girl Robert learned nothing but her name, Consuelo Alarid, and Skillman's feeling for her was suggested only in the way he spoke it.

When the trappers came back the town had been sacked by Apaches. With unsparing detail Skillman made him see the ruined plaza—the houses burned to smouldering adobe shells with roofs fallen in, the bodies of men lying naked, scalped and mutilated, and two babies dead in a cactus patch where they had been tossed alive. . . . Robert squirmed away from the picture but Skillman held him with a tightening powerful hand upon his knee as though under an urgent need to make someone share, however faintly, what he had seen and felt. . . . He gave a meticulous account with much topographical detail of trappers and Mexicans trailing Apaches for days across unwatered sand and rock, pressing them closer and closer, finding slaughtered horses half eaten, finding at last a dead Indian covered with the pimples and puss of smallpox caught from one of the captives. Finally they surprised a camp of the Indians on

[25]

top of the Candelario mountains, fired a volley
and charged, killed a few and sent the rest scattering. They found two of the captive women dead
and one of them, Skillman's girl, hanging naked
by her thumbs over a slow fire, roasting to death
as a sacrifice to Apache Gods who had sent the
scourge of smallpox. The girl was still alive and
looked Skillman in the eyes but could no longer
speak or scream and died when they cut her down.

When he had told this Skillman suddenly re-
leased Robert's knee, sat back in his chair and
wiped sweat off his face.

"Jesus!" he exclaimed.

After a few minutes of silence he rose wearily
and motioned with his head toward the bar.

"Come on, pard," he commanded. "Have a
drink!"

Robert rose and followed him to the bar and
stood there bewildered. It seemed as though Skillman's story had dissolved the walls of the room
and had let in the vast and hostile wilderness that
lay all about the town. He was suddenly, achingly
aware of the terror and cruelty of a country un-
subdued, where men and beasts lived by killing and
pity had never been born. He remembered the
slaughtered buffalo and antelope of the wagon
train, the blood and guts, the mules with festered
collar galls. He remembered a story one of the
drivers told him about a man who shot a Kiowa

squaw because Indians had killed his brother and how the Kiowa caught him and skinned him alive and he lived for over an hour that way . . . and another about a man they tied to a tree and stuck burning splinters of pitch pine into his flesh until he died. . . . He remembered the awful empty breadth of the prairie, buried now under darkness that hid a thousand violent deaths. . . . The room had seemed thick-walled and ample a moment before and now it shrank to a frail and tiny cube of light and order in a world of blackness, chaos and brutal death. . . .

With an effort he swallowed burning bad whisky, gagged on it but got it down. He took a second drink when Skillman did and then he began to feel a little better. Strangely, as his blood warmed, he felt himself transformed. A wretch in the face of destruction became the hero of a harrowing adventure. Sympathy for Skillman began to stir him tardily toward speech.

"That must have been . . . awful!" he remarked shyly.

Skillman turned on him as though just remembering he was there, looked him sadly up and down, turned away and walked slowly out of the room. Those sorrowful keen eyes with so much knowledge of life and death behind them made Robert feel as though he had been judged and found forever and hopelessly wanting.

As Skillman went out the door, Tom Foote looked up from his game.

"You better lock up, Jake," he said to Tolliver. "If he comes back he'll act bad."

"He's pretty full," Jake considered. "Maybe he'll go to bed."

Tom Foote shrugged and the room fell into silence.

In about fifteen minutes Skillman reappeared in the doorway with a long old fashioned six shooter cocked in his right hand. He waved it in a wide gesture.

"Close up this joint!" he commanded. "I'm gonna run this town!" Everybody sat still but Tolliver. He began taking glasses and bottles off the bar. Skillman stepped quickly over and smashed them with a sweeping blow of his gun. He turned and looked around the room.

"You Goddam lazy greasers settin' around here!" he suddenly roared. "You ain't never done nothin'. . . . A roomful of you ain't a mouthful for me!"

Heavy silence followed this. Skillman walked slowly to the door, turned and vaguely menaced Tolliver with his gun.

"Close up this joint!" he roared, "An don't stick your goddam head out till I tell you to . . ." He disappeared. Tolliver banged and locked the door behind him and began hastily closing shutters.

"It's your deal, Diego," Tom Foote reminded.

Robert looked down at his knuckles and saw them whitened by pressure against the arms of his chair . . . Tolliver seemed to think some explanation was due the stranger.

"Old Ed, he gets that way every once in so often," he said. "He jest comes all unglued. . . . But there ain't no harm in him. He never shoots unless it's at a bottle or something. He always pays the damages and he won't let nobody else shoot up this town. It's the peacefullest town in the country . . ."

Chapter Four

SUNDAY morning Robert sat in his room waiting for his hot bath.

He had bargained against all custom and pre-
cedent for hot water every Sunday. The irrigating
ditch that ran yellow at best and sometimes chocolate brown served as bath-tub and wash-tub for
most of the town and supplied drinking water.
Women dipped it up in tall pottery, carried it
home on their heads and set it to cool and clear
in breezy hallways. Only Doxey had water hauled
from the river in a hogshead on wheels and settled
in covered barrels.

Last time the old woman had brought his bath
but this morning her daughter, Maria, came staggering through the door with a steaming kettle in
one hand and a wooden tub in the other. She set
them down, straightened up, blew out her breath,
smoothed back her hair, and considered Robert
with a steady gaze and a wide smile.

"*Mucho trabjo!*" she exclaimed. Robert smiled
and nodded, delighted to hear words he knew. It
seemed to him a Mexican never turned a hand
without uttering that unctuous, "Much work!"

At this point the conversation paused for lack

of ideas and shared vocabularly but Maria continued to give him a look of unabashed pleasure that made him uncomfortable.

Although they were beautifully polite in every other way, poor Mexicans always stared at him. He knew this was partly because he had light wavy hair and grey eyes. Any kind of blond was still a rarity to most of them.

Maria was a wide-fashioned comely girl many shades lighter than her mother. The tint of her skin was almost golden and it looked well with her brown eyes and heavy black hair. She went barefoot about her housework and her dress was nothing more than a blue cotton smock but it was clean. Robert thought she was the best looking girl he had seen in the town where so many were squat and pitted. It gave him pleasure to look at her. She filled his eye, she filled his empty room. As she bent to pour steaming water, little silver beads of sweat stood out on her round brown neck, her deep breasts bagged her frock and her bent arm showed a smooth bulge of strength. . . . Although he liked to look at her he wished she would go now because he didn't know what to say. But she straightened up, gave him another long thoughtful look and began telling him something in Spanish of which he could understand nothing except that it concerned her mother.

"*No sabe,*" he told her sadly. He was getting

[31]

tired of saying that. . . . But Maria was deter-
mined to tell him something, and she went all over
it again, accompanying speech with gestures which
showed plainly her mother had gone to some distant spot, apparently across the river, for the
whole day. She then prodded herself in the breast
with one finger and embraced the premises in a
wide sweep of both arms, making it eloquently
clear, even if he had not understood the word
solo, that she was in the house all alone.

To this news she evidently attached some sig-
nificance Robert could not grasp. Bright-eyed with
expectancy, panting from her passionate effort to
make herself clear, she stood before him waiting,
almost demanding response. And he could think
of nothing to say and couldn't have said it anyway. He squirmed in his seat, forced a foolish
smile and sat staring at her bare brown dusty feet.

Disappointed, Maria picked up her kettle and
took herself slowly to the door where she stopped
and looked back at him for a moment. Then she
laughed, a little scornfully he thought, and went
away.

Robert was glad to see her go and at the same
time felt an impulse to run out and call her back.

After contact with strangers and especially with
women, he almost always had a feeling of embarrassed failure. He went and looked at himself in
the mirror and did not like his looks. Angel-face

he had been called at school and more than once he had fought but always as soon as he began to fight he began to cry and when you cried you were licked. They used to get girls to go and sit down beside him because that always made him blush.

When he had bathed and dressed he felt better and went across the placita and heard Maria singing in the kitchen. He stood outside the door for a moment trying to make up something good to say in Spanish but all he could remember was the greeting he had learned for use in the store. "How are you? How is your family? What do you want today?" That seemed inadequate, so he went back.

The rest of a long still sunny day he spent aridly alone, reading over letters from home. As he read them it seemed to him he was still back in Connecticut. His real self was like a person remembered, for he had left behind almost everything that had made him what he was. In this place he seemed to be nothing but an ache of loneliness and a conviction of futility.

The long sunny silence of the afternoon became worse than empty. It became oppressive. The quiet of lonely hours seemed a hush of suspense. He wandered restlessly around the room and peered uneasily out the window. Like a lost man he prickled with fear of the unknown. He had lost himself in a strange world, and dangerous undiscovered selves stirred faintly inside his skin.

[33]

Chapter Five

HE could add columns almost at a glance and his speed and skill at the books drove him out into the store. As soon as he saw he had no excuse to shirk it he went and stood behind the counter.

Mexicans were slow buyers. They turned a thing over and over in their hands, sometimes for five minutes, asked a price, thought a while, made an offer. There was an asking price and a selling price and a long slow haggle between. His duty was to sell as dear as he could and his impulse to sell for a fair profit, and he always did his duty with disgust.

A crowd of Mexicans from far up the valley came in and one of them discovered him and stood and stared, not asking anything, just looking. Others came and stood and looked. Black-shawled women stood behind blue-shirted men and stared and little dirty brown.children hid behind women's skirts and stared and one of them suddenly let a loud yell and earned a wallop on the ear.

"What do you want?" Robert demanded, blushing. They dropped their jaws. He pounded a nervous fist on the counter. "What do you want?"

His gray eyes burned anger in his reddened face. They went away and left him.

After a while a woman came back with a baby wrapped up in a shawl. She hesitated, came timidly forward, held out the bundle. "If you please, if you please . . ." she muttered. She opened her bundle and showed a baby with a red swollen face, like raw meat, dribbling saliva.

Old man Doxey, who always walked around watching, saw and came running. He chased the woman away with rapid furious Spanish, expostulated to her husband, drove the whole family out of the store. Then he came back and explained.

"That kid's got scarlet fever, sure as hell. . . . They think you're some kind of a holy healer that can cure anything with a touch. . . . Any man with light hair, kind of long. . . . There's several long-haired humbugs go through the country every summer, touching sick people and gathering up everything they can carry. You look kind of like one of 'em. . . . After they get used to seeing you they won't bother you no more."

Late in the day Maria came in and stood before him just as she had when she brought his bath, and gave him the same bright hopeful smile. She wore shoes and stockings, and a sun bonnet, and did not look nearly so formidable as she had with naked arms and legs. This and his businesslike entrenchment behind a counter made him feel more at ease and he recited his greeting and his challenge to buy with a certain authority.

Maria wanted soap—that much he could understand—but what kind of soap could be learned only by trial and error. All the kinds of soap in the store he brought one by one and each Maria examined carefully, deliberately, above all each she smelt critically and each returned with a sweet tender smile.

Finally he brought toilet soap with a perfume that would have made it easy to find in the dark. It seemed to him a most unsuitably expensive soap for Maria to buy, but she greeted it with joy, inhaled it with ecstasy closing her eyes, untied many knots in a handkerchief and counted out small coins, paying the first price he asked.

He felt as though he were robbing the poor, taking food out of her mouth, but she went away with her soap, beaming, and threw him a last shining smile of gratitude before she went out the door.

Tom Foote noted the departing smile and gave a wink.

"Nice little *muchacha* . . . she must like you," he remarked.

Robert hid blushes putting soap on shelves.

"My landlady's daughter," he explained.

"That makes it handy," said Tom Foote.

"You'd never think she was the old woman's daughter," said Robert to show he was unflustered.

"Not the same color. . . . No," Foote answered. "She's a child of the old French priest they had here till a few years ago when Bishop Lamey chased him out. . . . At least so the old woman claims and I guess she's right. He had quite a few and all the women are proud of 'em. If you praise up the girl to the old woman she'll tell you. . . . They considered it an honor to have a child by the padre. They thought a lot of that old man. He was a padre more ways than one. He done what he could to breed up the stock."

When he sat in the plaza that evening Maria passed by with another girl. She smiled· at him and said something to the other, and both of them looked back and smiled, turned away and giggled, looked back and smiled again. Robert grinned uneasily and looked himself over, wondering if he had spilled egg on his shirt or forgotten to shave. Then he noticed that other girls smiled over their shoulders at other men. . . . The whole town flirted that way in the evening. He felt unexpectedly warmed and pleased. He stretched his legs and lit his pipe. A smile had pulled him down from painful heights of isolation, made him one of a row of idle squatting fellows watching girls go by. . . .

Chapter Six

Now that he had proved his value to the store by holding his own with the books and behind the counter, Doxey bade him to supper. It was an honor and he knew it, for Doxey and his family were exclusive to almost the whole of the town.

Sweating inside his best black stock he sat on haircloth in Doxey's Missouri-Baptist sitting room, with its imported carpet and white lace curtains, sea-shells under glass bells, family album and twelve-dollar Bible on a little bowlegged table, embroidered motto about God, brand new Packard organ hauled a thousand miles by wagon. . . . Doxey's sitting room made no compromise with race or country.

Three Doxey women in high collars, tight bodices and fourteen yards of skirt apiece spoke properly of weather, wished for rain, eyed him with eyes that hid interesting thoughts. Mrs. Doxey wore steel-rimmed spectacles pushed up on steel gray hair and a long row of little cloth-covered buttons marched way up and over a vast black silk bosom.

Addie and Caddie the girls were called. Addie was young and plump, with a weak, pretty still-hopeful mouth. Caddie was of an age never to be guessed, with restless hands, lean wrists and dark questing eyes beginning to doubt. Doxey, who was everything in the store, here was nothing but a gray beard hiding a silent mouth. Only when they sat down to table he modestly asked God to make them all truly grateful.

Robert truly was, for here were chicken and dumplings, mashed potatoes and snap beans, hot biscuits and lemon pie. Over last cups of coffee all felt more at ease in the solidarity of being full and satisfied. Robert got out something about so glad to be here, so much like home. . . . .Old lady Doxey took this for a cue, said she felt it her first duty to make a home in this wild barbarous country for husband and daughters such as they might have had back in the states. It was an awful sacrifice for women, for young girls especially—but it seemed to be the will of God—to live in this faraway place where were no refinement, no culture, no religion even except a degenerate Romanism.

"They have no morals out here, not even the priests. . . . I just can't tell you . . . unspeakable!"

Much here a lady could not speak but she could make it clear to Robert that she offered him refuge from an evil world, with chicken for dinner and prayers and hymns on Sunday.

Doxey disappeared first and then Mrs. Doxey.

[39]

Addie and Caddie sat on either side of him showing him pictures in an album. A voice summoned
Addie and she went away but came back in a little
while and sat down closer, rumpling her skirt
against his knee. He murmured politely over pictures, seeing the girls only as hands. A lean hard
restless hand flicked pages and a smaller plump
soft hand touched moistly his own.

A voice again summoned Addie and this time
she did not come back but in a long pause of feeble
talk he heard a distant sob that Caddie quickly
smothered in words.

"Do you think you'll ever like it out here?" she
asked him. "I know I never will. Ever since I came
back from St. Louis it's been so lonely. . . . There's
no one, absolutely no one, a lady can associate with.
. . . I was so glad when I saw you!"

The human honesty of that last lifted his eyes
to hers with his thanks.

Across a wide stiff barrier of Crinoline he looked
into timidly hopeful eyes. She had a thin mouth
with dry cracked lips and cheeks a little lean. She
flushed, and both of them looked down again at
pictures. . . .

Robert was glad to be out in the plaza and alone
once more. He pulled off his stock to cool his neck,
walked over to the store and sat down on his
familiar bench, puffed a pipe and stretched his legs,
glad of solitude. He was glad the evening had gone

off so well and hoped there would not be another one like it very soon.

A couple of young Mexicans, boy and girl, passed without seeing him, much engrossed in each other. They played like puppies, pushing and laughing. They were going his way and he rose and followed them, feeling guilty. He saw their play end in a hard embrace, heard the girl slap her man and laugh. . . . It gave him a curious lonely thrill.

He entered the hall as quietly as he could but evidently his footsteps were heard for a door opened beside him and Maria spoke.

"*Quien es?*" she asked.

When he answered her proudly in Spanish she laughed.

"You come late," she said.

"Yes," he answered and stood awkwardly, thinking how Maria turned up everywhere. She watched his comings and goings. None but he could wait on her in the store. He felt as he had when a stray pup elected to follow him—flattered but also embarrassed. With stray pups and brown girls he didn't know how to deal.

She stood within a yard of him, a whitish blur and a faint feminine alien odor, not unpleasant, mixed with perfume of soap he had sold. She laughed again, uneasily.

His hand went toward her and he drew it back again, frightened, wondering what his hand had

[41]

intended. He wanted to speak but he could think of nothing to say except "Good-night." As he stumbled across the placita he could feel his cheeks burning in the dark. He heard again Maria's mocking giggle and slammed his door emphatically to drown it out.

Chapter Seven

A HIGH wind blew from the West, yellow with flying sand, blurring the shapes of houses and mountains, filling the town with rattle of loose shutters, bang of doors and curses of irritated men with sand in their eyes and mouths. Everyone ate sand and breathed sand. Everyone hated the wind. It ruined tempers and brought on quarrels.

To make this one worse it blew in from the West a band of Navajos who camped in the plaza and came to the store to trade. Doxey hastily planted guards on the porch and in the store for Navajos would steal and always might start trouble. They were tall handsome men with hair twisted into queues of red wool, and blue dabs of turquoise in their ears.

They piled the counters with the heavy blankets their women wove in bold patterns of black and red and white, with silver and turquoise jewelry and with soft-tanned gray and tawney pelts. They wore knives in their belts and Mexicans walked wide of their scornful looks. Tom Foote openly wore a long Colt and looked formidable as any warrior, being over six feet in his boots.

"I almost wish some of these bucks would start

something," he remarked to Robert. "I'm gettin' horney for trouble. This store-keepin' makes me sick. Nothin' ever happens. I was on the road three years and Doxey got me in here because I can talk good Mex and know the people. He give me more money and all that but I can't stand it much longer. If I had a little more I'd start out on my own."

Robert could see he had something more to say but business interrupted just then.

That night in Tolliver's Tom came and sat down beside him and they had a drink together.

"What brought you here, Pard?" Tom wanted to know. "It ain't none of my business but you don't look as if you belonged."

Robert considered a minute.

"I wanted to make more money," he explained at last. "I couldn't make anything back East."

This seemed to give Tom an opening he wanted.

"You can't make none settin' around here neither," he said earnestly. "If a man stays around these little towns he jest goes greaser himself. He gets him a Mexican girl and she don't egg him on like a white woman would. He lickers up when he likes and nobody minds. It's a lazy country and it makes a man lazy. When everything comes easy you jest rot. . . . The only way to make any money out here is to go tradin' on your own and if I had a pardner and a little more money that's what I'd do."

He gave Robert a long thoughtful look while he rolled a cigarette with one hand, licked it shut and lit it.

"I ain't makin' you no proposition jest yet," he went on. "But I been thinkin'. . . . I can see you're on the level and that's what counts with me. More'n half these bozos out here is crooked as a dog's hind leg. You're slick with the books, too, and I can hardly figger at all. But I know mules and Mexicans. The two of us might make a pullin' team . . ."

He held up a hand as Robert began to flush and sputter.

"Don't say nothin' now. Jest think it over. Old Papa Doxey ain't gonnna give you nothin' to take back home."

Tom walked away leaving Robert proud but bewildered. He didn't know what to think. He couldn't believe anybody in this country would want him for a partner. He wondered if Tom thought he had money, felt as though he ought to hurry over and explain he hadn't a hundred dollars to his name. . . . But no . . . not now . . . wait and see. Warmed by liquor and kind words he sat comfortably puffing his pipe, feeling vaguely important.

After a little while young Diego came in, slammed the door, damned the wind and stood looking around the room with eager restless eyes.

[45]

Robert watched him uneasily, as he always did. He could never keep his eyes off the young Mexican. In the plaza he was always watching Diego's easy way with girls and horses, always aware of his graceful supple strength, his untroubled lazy laugh. And Diego always made him think of all that stood behind the man—of the great Aragon house he had never entered and the sheep by tens of thousands and the horses and the peons and the silver. Take all that away from him and what would be left of Diego? Nothing! He didn't know how to work. . . . Looking at Diego, Robert felt always small and inadequate, but he also felt within himself an immense capacity for patient toil.

Diego didn't look his way and never had. There was nothing pointed in his neglect, either. He seemed to be simply unaware of Robert's existence.

The young Mexican walked to the bar and drank two of his favorite white grape brandies in rapid succession. That probably meant it was one of his rare drunken nights for he was ordinarily moderate. He challenged Tom to a game of two-handed stud, there being no other players present, and after a little surly hesitation Tom agreed. They settled down to silent play and Robert forgot about them. His unaccustomed drink was making him sleepy. He sat with half closed eyes barely keeping his pipe alight, aware of nothing but the taste of tobacco and the voice of the wind.

Raised angry voices brought him out of stupor. He saw through blinking lids that Tom and Diego were quarrelling. Over Diego's shoulder he saw Tom's face red and ugly, with blue eyes glinting battle, and he saw fear in the tension of Tolliver's long back as he leaned across the bar watching. . . .

"Liar!" The word cracked like a gun. Diego dived across the table and two men and a chair went to the floor with a crash. Foote was the bigger man but the fall seemed to stun him. As Robert came to his feet he could see that Diego had Tom pinned and was hammering at his head. Blood he could see on a twisting rolling face. He rushed toward them, his own hands clenching hard, his heart pounding painfully, filled with a sudden new excitement he didn't understand. . . .

Tolliver caught him from behind, and pushed him toward the door.

"It won't do for you to horn in," he said hastily. "Run and call Doxey quick. Them boys'll ruin each other. . . ."

When Robert came back with Doxey the fight was over. Old Don Aragon apparently had come in and stopped it, for he had backed his son into a corner and held him there firmly with a grip on his shirt. The Don was a small man with white hair and white moustache, but the much taller son took a furious scolding in rapid Spanish with an expression like a small boy about to be spanked. When it was over he slunk scowling through the door. The Don made courtly apology to Tolliver for the trouble his child had caused, offered to pay any damages and bowed himself out.

Tom Foote sat in a corner mopping blood off his face with a large red handkerchief. Doxey went to him, laid a hand on his arm and began talking to him in a low tone. Tom shook him off and got up.

"I'm gonna get my gun," he announced. "That Goddam greaser'll be huntin' me with his. . . ." They went out together, Doxey still arguing.

Tolliver, left alone with Robert, was excited and full of talk. He evidently enjoyed the situation and was worried about it at the same time.

"You never want to try to stop a fight in these parts," he cautioned Robert. "It's bad manners. Only the old Don could do it. I run and told him right away. A Mexican's father is Godalmighty to him as long as he lives. I've seen 'em spank a kid twenty years old. . . ."

"Well, I'm glad it's over," Robert said. He filled and lit a pipe to cover his own excitement and hoped Tolliver didn't notice his unsteady hand.

"Yes, but I'm afraid it ain't," Tolliver told him. "Tom's gone for his gun and Diego may do the same, if he ain't too drunk. They're the best kind of friends, too, but that ain't gonna keep 'em from killin' each other when they get this way. Tom gets a fightin' streak every oncet in so often, especially when the wind blows, and Diego's got a hair-trigger temper. He's killed a few Indians and that don't make him no better. Them Mexicans jest drink blood. They love to see it, every one of 'em."

"Can't we do anything to keep them apart?" Robert enquired, feeling less calm and judicious than he sounded.

Tolliver shrugged.

"What kin we do?" he asked. "If either of 'em comes here I'm gonna close up. I ain't gonna stand for no gunplay." He thought a minute, eyeing Robert. "Tell you what you might do," he suggested. "You might go over to Archuletta's place on the other side of the plaza. It's the only other place in town that's open. Either of 'em might go there to get liquored up—especially Diego. He practically owns Archuletta and he can do anything he pleases over there. If either of 'em shows up, you come tell me."

Robert went, a little dubious, and sat down in Archuletta's dirty saloon. It was furnished with an old wooden counter and a bench and table against a wall patterned like a spider web with cracked white plaster. Fat dirty Archuletta, asleep in a corner, woke at a step and served wine in drowsy surprise. Robert sat uneasily, sipping and waiting. The longer he sat the more uneasy he felt. His excitement was all oozing out of him now. For a moment he had felt like jumping into that fight and now he was scared at the recollection of his own mad impulse. That would have been a hell of a thing to do! And what was he sitting here for? What would he say if Diego did come in? He wished he was out of there, but he couldn't quite make up his mind to a shameless retreat. He looked at his watch. Twenty minutes he would wait and then go back and tell Tolliver Diego hadn't showed up. . . .

Diego came in quietly and stood staring at Robert with suspicious hostile eyes. On a heavy wide belt sagging over his right hip he wore a great pearl-handled Colt in a carved leather holster, easily as though it had grown there, fingers just brushing the butt as he moved. . . . Robert felt as though his insides had dropped about a foot.

Diego jerked a thumb at the bar and invited Robert to drink, with a somewhat sarcastic politeness. Robert cleared his throat.

"No thanks," he said. "I must go. . . ."

Diego jerked a more urgent thumb and his fingers played around the pearl handle. Robert rose and walked to the bar. He ordered wine. Diego, never letting the bottle out of his hand, took drink upon drink of straight brandy. After the fifth drink he turned to Robert.

"Did you ever see a man killed, companero?" he asked quietly. He looked at Robert with terrible eyes. "Come with me and you will see a man killed," he said.

He took Robert firmly by the arm and led him out into the dark. The wind still whooped and blew sand in their eyes. Robert walked with weak knees. . . .

Diego stopped and turned on him suddenly, drawing his gun.

"Are you with me, companero?" he demanded.

Robert felt that his life depended on playing a part. He cleared his throat and tried to speak heartily.

"Sure!" he said. "Let's go. . . ."

"*Bueno . . . vamos!*" Diego agreed. They turned to face the wind again.

Robert laid a hand on Diego's arm. He could feel the man rock as he walked. . . . Diego was pretty drunk. . . . A cunning desperate plan filled Robert's head. He steered Diego ever so gently toward the *ace'quia madre,* the big ditch that ran through the town. There was a path along the bank of it.

Fearful but resolute he guided Diego's stumbling steps into the path along the ditch. . . . With the spasmodic nervous energy of the scared he hooked a leg about both of Diego's and pushed. . . .

They hit the ditch together head first. Robert held his breath and got to his feet immediately, standing in mud and water a little over his knees. Of Diego he saw nothing but a large white hat floating rapidly away. He plunged fumbling frantic arms into the water, got hold of his man, water-logged and incredibly heavy . . . heaved, pushed, dragged, got him at last against the bank, running rivulets, plastered with mud, barely conscious.

Diego, taking no notice· of him, first coughed, snorted, blew each nostril clear, holding the other with a finger, then sat gasping and helpless. He felt for his hat. He felt for his gun. Both gone!

A long moment he sat silent, then turned to Robert and spoke huskily.

"Companero, promise me . . . never to tell anyone . . . never tell anyone this and I am your friend for life!"

Robert sat weak, thinking what if Diego had drowned! Then he would have killed a man! Death had been all around . . . was gone now. Robert sat limp with relief. It took him a little while to realize all Diego wanted was a promise no one should ever know he had fallen into a ditch! When he understood he put out a limp wet muddy hand and in mud they sealed the agreement.

Diego sighed.

"I was very drunk," he remarked. "Now I am sober. How did we fall in the ditch, companero?"

"I don't know," Robert told him. "We were both very drunk."

Diego presently got to his feet.

"Good-night, companero," he said. They went damply squishing their separate ways.

Chapter Eight

THE next day Diego came into the store, smiling dapper and new-hatted. Robert in amazement saw him make up with Tom. They stood laughing and chatting for ten minutes, seemingly better friends than ever. Then Diego came over to Robert and held out his hand. He gave a wide smile and a warm easy grip.

"Companero," he said. "You must come to supper with me to-night. You must come to my house. My house is yours."

Robert blushed and muttered thanks. He felt warmed and pleased and he also felt somehow small and limited before this strong brown man with the gleaming white teeth who could be so many things in so short a time and each so completely.

He puzzled over Diego all day. He could not comprehend such a man. Did Diego know what had happened or had he been too drunk to understand? Was Diego really grateful to Robert, or merely afraid he would tell? And he had been invited to Aragon's for supper. . . . He wanted to go and yet was afraid to knock on that formidable door.

Diego dispelled his fears by coming for him when the store closed and leading him home by the arm.

Diego wanted to learn English. He spoke a little but he wanted to learn it well. Robert must teach him English. They must go hunting together. They were friends—more, they were brothers!

Overwhelmed by this sudden warmth, wholly unable to make any adequate response, Robert was led to the house of Aragon and saw with timid interest what was behind its mighty walls and iron-barred windows.

It was gaudy with all the spoil of the wagon trade—red carpet an inch deep in the *sala,* red curtains held in great brass rings, blue plush chairs and sofas, immensely overstuffed, and all around the walls gilt-framed mirrors that multiplied its magnificence. It did not look as though anyone had ever lived in it or ever could. Robert felt ill-at-ease and hardly dared sit down. But old Don Aragon and his fat wife quickly made him feel better. Never had he been greeted with such kindly perfect courtesy. "My house is yours," the Don told him and bowed and pressed his hand with a manner that was perfectly formal and yet seemed warm and spontaneous as a kiss. . . . The Dona spoke no English but her beaming placid smile was worth more than words.

Neither of them had ever looked at him before

[55]

but now that chance had brought him inside their house he was that sacred thing, a guest. He was the pleased though flustered center of the family.

Besides the parents and Diego, there was a married daughter home on a visit, Dona Martinez of Taos, young but fat already, and an unmarried daughter, Nina, slim and pretty, just out of a St. Louis convent. When she came in she bowed to her parents as to monarchs, smiled timidly upon the guest and sat in virginal silence, looking too innocent for any human use. Her luscious young prettiness and the angelic remoteness of her expression made for Robert a fascinating combination. He glanced at her as often as he dared and she glanced back and even once faintly smiled. . . . Then came in with a great bustle of hearty greeting a rotund polished-brown young man with a waxy-black moustache and sharp dark eyes—a heavy man but light and quick on his small neatly-booted feet. All of the family embraced him in turn, the Don hammering him lustily on the back, the two older women taking him placidly to their large bosoms. Lastly he seized the so-virginal Nina in his arms and smacked loud kisses on her flushed cheeks while she averted her mouth. Robert blushed painfully, feeling as though he saw a child ravished before his eyes. But this, he learned, was Nina's fiance, Don Salomon Ortiz, who would marry her in a month. She had been promised to him by her parents before she went away to school.

Supper here was merry and washed down with much red wine. Only the men spoke English and Robert's Spanish was still too weak for general conversation, but Don Ortiz translated for the ladies and all made Robert feel that his few and timid words were most important. He could feel wine climbing up into his ears and knew he wore a foolish happy look. Often his eyes met the smile of Dona Aragon, warmly motherly, making him feel young but safe. . . . All Mexican women, he had noticed, seemed to be full of a surplus tenderness that looked for something to spend itself upon. Although they had so many children they were always adopting orphans and they raised motherless lambs on the bottle for good measure. He remembered sharply by contrast the looks of the Doxey women, so keen and disturbing, hiding so much. The smiles of these soft prolific untroubled mothers seemed to contain all they were.

After supper all played merry childish games— drop the handkerchief and blind man's buff and another one strange to him in which each tried to bite a bullet off a precarious pyramid of flour without mussing up his face. Dignified Don Aragon played a surprising graceful part in all this and glowed and beamed with unctuous family feeling, and even the fat Dona wore a blindfold and clasped

Robert in her enormous arms. Then he went groping with bandaged eyes, and saw from under the
fold the unfleeing feet of Nina. He caught her and
held her a bold thrilling moment before he spoke
her name. They stood covered with pink young
confusion while the others laughed and applauded.
This was charming, everyone seemed to think, even
Don Ortiz. . . . Robert had never felt so warm
and happy.

They had cakes and wine again before he went
home and this time he found himself striding
across the plaza, feeling as though at each step he
might leave the earth. He felt happy and full of
power and above all free. Wine and laughter and
friendly hands and eyes had cracked his shell and
set him free.

Go to bed he could not. He wanted to talk and
shake hands. He would have liked to dance if he
had known how. He wanted someone to listen to
him, someone to touch. . . .

He went to Tolliver's because he knew no place
else to go and found Skillman and the Judge playing a sleepy game of seven-up while Tom and a
stranger stood at the bar chatting over a leisurely
drink. He went up to Tom and shook hands with
him warmly, as though just back from a long
journey. Surprised, Tom introduced the other.
Robert slammed a silver dollar on the bar.

[58]

"Have one on me," he invited, pushing his hat back from a hot red brow. Tom grinned at him.

"Say, pardner, you're way up in the pictures to-night," he observed.

Robert gulped his drink, took Tom by the arm and led him aside.

"You remember what you said. . . . We'd go trading. . . . Well, anywhere, anytime. . . . Count on me!"

"All right, old man," Tom told him. "I do count on you. . . . You look about fourteen when you're full and nothin' any greener ever growed but you're on the level and you kin learn." He steered Robert to the door. "I got a deal on with this mule skinner now. You run on home to your little playmate."

Robert started homeward again, feeling at first a little let down, but the swing of walking and the wine in his blood soon restored his all-conquering mood.

At the door Maria had opened before he found himself standing expectant. He coughed loudly but nothing stirred. . . . Maria had turned up so often when he had been unable to think of a word to say. . . . Now he was full of words, in two languages and craved human contact as never before. He lifted his hand and gently knocked. He watched himself do this in surprise at his own daring. He knocked again and harder. With a jump of the blood, like a hunter starting game, he heard a creak and rustle and soft quick-padding steps of bare feet.

"Who is it?" she asked as she opened the door a little.

For answer he laughed and put out a hand. She took it and opened the door wider and drew him in, sniffing his breath.

"My drunken one, my little drunken one!" she murmured tenderly.

He could not see her. She was but warm flesh forming under his hands. She was the fruit of his new-found mood. His needing hands seemed to mould a woman out of the dark. . . .

Chapter Nine

SEPTEMBER was turning the valley yellow when they started. The trip had been planned in June and they should have been on the road in July but this was a Mexican expedition.

Tom had talked it to him for months. Against many doubts and drawbacks he had brought himself to give up a good job, buy a horse and a mule and put all the rest of his savings into scarlet cloth, glass beads, knives and lead.

This morning he hardly knew himself. His own destiny seemed incredible. . . . Booted and spurred, with a carbine under his leg, he rode toward mountains so faintly blue they seemed no part of the earth.

He rode with eager wonder but not without regret. Another life he was leaving and he was surprised how sweet it seemed—long peaceful days in the store, evenings of wine and tobacco with Tom and Diego, nights of a desire slowly burning down, shame and lust turning into tenderness and habit. . . . That he had been happy only struck him now that he was going away. . . . Those evenings at the Aragons, too, and his long timid flirtation with Nina, and her wedding which brought together such an impressive gathering of rich Mexican relatives in Concord coaches, and lasted with music and feasting all of a day and a night. He remembered best Nina's bewildered tear-stained face peering through the window of the coach that carried her away. He had come to understand that Nina's marriage united important families and large tracts of land, and it spread a mild romantic sadness over his life for weeks.

The only sharp pain he remembered was getting letters from Elizabeth . . . long finely penned letters all about devotion unchanging and the goodness of God and her loneliness. Pain twisted him in his chair when he sat down to answer for Elizabeth was only half real now. The more his new life absorbed him the fainter became that memory of golden hair and Annie Laurie. . . . She was not real but his promise was real, and so was the guilt that bit him whenever he thought of her.

Each letter was a pang but it did not last long. He was learning how the flesh well served cushions the spirit, how peaceful days and easy satisfactions make everything remote but what the hand touches. . . . Yet from the moment Tom proposed the trip, although he hesitated, his peace was doomed. He didn't know why but he couldn't refuse.

They were going West and South by way of Acoma and Zuni. Some mules and horses they might buy cheap from the Pueblos but the main destination was a great camp of Apaches somewhere in the Gila country. The Apaches were at peace, as much as ever they were. They had been raiding across the Rio Grande in Old Mexico and their camp was full of stolen mules and horses. They wanted to trade and would trade cheap— that was the news. Horses and mules bought from Apaches for next to nothing in trade goods would sell for hard silver money in Santa Fe. Then he and Tom would buy a wagon.

Tom had their fortunes made over and over again in eager excited talk. . . . If the Indians didn't get bad. . . . If the snows didn't fall too early. . . .

He couldn't assess these hazards and he didn't try. In him simply a longing to cling to warm flesh and easy ways fought unsuccessfully against an impulse to move, risk, suffer, win big or lose all. Out of peace and satiety this wild venture had sprouted like a plant out of deep rich soil.

Mounted and riding, the farther he went the more he was glad he had come. He sat high and his big grey mare was lively between his knees.

Cottonwood trees along the river where the frost bit first were already bright butter yellow and goldenrod was yellow beside the road. Half-tended orchards sagged under the red weight of small hard apples, grapes showed a dusty purple through

[63]

the leaves of low bushy vineyards and scarlet strings of drying chile hung from the rafter-ends of all the houses.

Scarlet purple and golden the valley lay about him. . . . He had never seen it beautiful before.

Men picking fruit, gathering melons, driving ponies round threshing floors stopped work to wish them luck. Women in doorways waved them adios with wide sweeps of blackshawled arms.

For the first time he was aware of the valley, not as a place faroff and strange but sweetly familiar. Fruit had ripened since he came here. . . . He had bitten ripe fruit . . .

Their cavalcade gathered slowly along fourteen miles of valley road. When they climbed the sandhills there were nineteen men and boys, and about forty horses, mules and burros straggled in a long train and raised a great pale dust cloud.

This was a community expedition which any might join. Robert and Tom were the only gringos.

They carried the only breech-loading arms and that made them more than welcome. Some of the Mexicans had old nine-pound Hawkin rifles, some smooth bore muskets they called *escopetas*, one had an old-fashioned bell-mouthed buffalo gun with a tasselled stopper in its muzzle. . . . For a Mexican expedition this was strong.

Old Miguel Romero carried only an Apache bow and arrows but he could knock a bird out of a tree with it and had killed deer at sixty paces. He rode a wonderful single-footing burro, guiding him with sharp swats of a short club, and drove two other burros loaded with outfit and trade goods. His long iron-gray hair was bound with a strip of red wool and he wore moccasins. His moustache was crinkly like a Chinaman's. He was half Navajo in blood but wholly Mexican in manner and speech.

The very first day he and Robert became *companeros* by reason of a shared taste for philosophical reflection and historical reminiscence.

Miguel's comment on everything deplorable was to shake his head and say, "So goes the world, Juana." His mind was a mass of lore, of traditional wisdom, of saws and sayings in prose and verse, of old unwritten songs. Half a savage, he was yet wholly a peasant of an ancient earth-cherishing strain.

Miguel had gone on a trading trip every year for thirty years. Formerly he had always joined the great *conducta* that used to gather at Socorro and travel South to trade home-woven woolen goods for chocolate, oranges, coffee, silks and silver. But now, in a world overwhelmed by change, the Sonorans got all they wanted by wagon from Santa Fe and from the Texas ports, so he went dangerously trading with wild Indians. For what would life be without trips? A man couldn't sit against the wall all the time. His women would get tired of seeing him there. Of course, what women would do when men were away! . . . So goes the world, Juana . . . Navajos were bad and Apaches were worse but Miguel put his faith in prayer, in penance and in candles that burned for the glory of his soul. At the same time his small deep-set eye missed no cloud of smoke, no fresh track in the road.

Miguel was a veteran of the war with the United States and he told Robert the story of his life in battle. . . . When the gringo columns marched on Taos, a fierce-looking Mexican dragoon came riding to Miguel's little rancho and told him it was ordered that all able-bodied men turn out to fight. Miguel explained he had to irrigate the chile crop and besides his wife was sick. The dragoon said all men who did not fight that day would be stood against a wall and shot. So Miguel took his bow and arrows and his best serape, mounted his burro and put out for the front.

He saw the gringo soldiers in a long row on a hilltop, he saw a gun on wheels spout a cloud of smoke as big as any cloud in the sky and its voice shook the mountains and rolled in the canyon with a noise like a hundred guns. Miguel's burro thereupon turned and started for home with a speed he had never shown before. Miguel went with him for a while but the burro, passing under a low tree, left Miguel on the ground. Even so he beat the burro home.

"When I got there," said Miguel, "my wife said to me, 'Where is your new serape?' I didn't know. I couldn't remember. It cost me eleven pesos. . . . When a man goes to war he should never take his best serape." Miguel shook a deploring head. "So goes the world, Juana."

For days they passed through a land of high flat mesas and little round hills thinly spotted with bunchy dark green cedar bushes. The rains of late summer had brought good grass out of the ground —thick green buffalo grass in low places and a thin tinge of nourishing purple gramma on the hills. Water was in rare springs and in seepage pools along the beds of sandy arroyos.

After the first day Robert rode less jauntily, for the unaccustomed saddle took skin off his tender bottom. He squirmed and shifted in his seat and felt as if his very bones were being laid bare. His back ached and he had cramps in his knees and ankles. He was glad when they camped.

Mexicans were neat and efficient campers. In no time stock was unpacked and unsaddled, mules and horses were gratefully rolling sweaty backs in the dirt and cropping grass with quick eager munches, fires of cedar and pinon snapped and crackled, meat sizzled against hot iron and coffee gurgled in the pot. Robert tried desperately to help and generally bungled. He finally chose for his lot to be a hewer of wood and a drawer of water. He had no comprehension of the nature and wants of mules and he could not solve the mystery of a squaw hitch, but he could demolish a dead tree with a certain perspiring ferocity and he could carry sloshing heavy buckets from distant waterholes. His greenness was understood and politely allowed for and he was called *El Joven.* . . .

Nights were already chilly. A windbreak of cedar brush was built with a fire before it. Almost always young Juan Guiterrez brought out his home-made guitar and strummed and sang short ditties and long ballads. All of them in minor keys and sadly told stories of romantic and disappointed love. Sometimes others joined in the singing. All had small husky voices that tended toward falsetto but they sang in perfect time and their music seemed of a piece with the sound of a night wind blowing over barren hills. . . . In a vast empty wilderness they sang sadly of lovely ladies and broken hearts, of firesides and dances.

Juan Guiterrez was twenty-one, handsome and in love. He was an unofficial troubadour to the party and a poet and improviser of recognized gifts. He could make up a couplet or a quatrain about anyone or anything that happened. When Tom Foote accidentally kicked over a pot of beans this event was memorialized in a song that won much applause. But Juan was at his best when he sang of passion. This trip, if he was lucky, would make him enough to marry. When he sang of aching hearts and shining eyes he almost choked. . . .

One by one men threw away last cigarette butts, spread sheep skins and heavy Indian blankets and lay down. The fire sank to a dull red glow that still threw up now and then a shadow-shaking spurt of flame.

The first few nights Robert couldn't sleep. The ground was too hard and too many strange noises filled the dark. Often he heard the coyotes yapping to each other from far apart in the evening, and he heard them again in a shrill chorus just before dawn. He thought much, and as once before he thought mostly of a woman. When he left her, Maria had become a thing of familiar convenience but now she appeared to him as a vision tormentingly voluptuous. . . . Now that he had known woman a part of him belonged to woman, he felt the weight of a chain he would always drag. . . . He remembered tenderly the night of his fall and the moment of guilt and shame that had followed. He had drunk wine to forget and filled with wine had fallen again into waiting arms. . . . With a twinge of humiliation he remembered how her mother had come to him demanding money, as was the custom of the country, and how he had found himself incredibly counting out clinking silver in payment for the body of a woman.

How many things he had done that seemed alien to himself! The country was making him over. He was in a fair way to become a good Mexican. He didn't know what to make of himself. He was full of sin and shame but also full of life. A due remorse was always being lost in a new sensation.

After a proper arrangement had been made, both of the women waited on him like slaves and Maria wept when he told her he was going away. She wept like a child deprived of its candy and smiled and dried her eyes when he gave her an eight-sided California golden ounce worth sixteen dollars.

After a few nights on the road, weariness overpowered both desire and regret and he began to sleep heavily. Each morning he mounted and rode with a greater zest as his skin conquered saddle leather and his muscles learned their work.

He rode long hours half awake, lulled by the sun and the jog of his horse, and when they topped high places and wide sudden views fell at his feet, he rode with a delight of discovery, as of a man

entering a new world and leaving everything behind.

They reached a country where sheer-walled mesas jutted up from the desert, sharp as bootheels,
and they climbed one of them to visit the pueblo
of Acoma, perched like a hunted squirrel on top of
its tall barren rock.

The friendly Indians came swarming down lad-
ders to greet visitors. Of Mexicans they were barely tolerant but they gathered in crowds to stare
at the two men with light eyes and blond hair.
They offered to trade all sorts of goods nobody
wanted but they had few horses to spare. A caci-
que, who looked a hundred years old, gravely
assigned them a house, and then came a procession
of brown women with bright blankets hooded over
their heads and legs enormously swathed in buckskin, bringing bread and meat, dried melons and
tinajas of precious far-carried water.

Beyond Acoma, Robert scratched his initials on
the bald red face of inscription rock alongside the
strange hieroglyphs of Spanish conquerors and
felt absurdly bumptious as he did it.

They went into a higher country now, most of
it a level mesa timbered with dwarf pine, gnarled
ancient pinons, and great blue fragrant cedar
bushes, shapely as Indian jugs. This woodland
was still and shady and grateful to the eyes after
so much glaring sunbaked distance.

Narrow rivers of dead lava, twisted and fretted as though they had cooled the day before, barred their paths and lamed their horses. They peered into some strange lava caves where ice lived all the year around and the air was cold as death. . . . For the first time now they saw much game. Bands of antelope wheeled and ran across the open places and in the woods tall gray deer with enormous ears bounced out of sight in long stiff-legged jumps. One stopped to look, a rifle cracked and it fell kicking. . . . When Robert saw red meat that night for the first time in twenty days and smelt liver sizzling in a pan he slavered with hunger. . . . He no longer shrank from blood.

At the great pueblo of Zuni they were welcomed and feasted again and housed in dark adobe rooms. Robert saw the famous family of Albino Indians that had always been among the Zuni. A skinny young buck over six feet tall with tow-white hair, a sickly yellow freckled face and watery blue eyes came forward and grasped him by the hand and called him brother in good Spanish. With his new-found brother he went up a ladder and down into a little stuffy room with gypsum-white walls where a squaw, colored like her spouse, tended a fire, and little dirty albino children crawled and ran about the floor. They were afraid of him at first and piled up in a corner like frightened puppies, but after a while they came and took hold of his clothes with tiny hands and reached up and touched his yellow whiskers which had sprouted an inch long. He ate stewed venison out of an earthen pot with his fingers. He felt hot and uncomfortable in the room, and pleased that these people, so strange they seemed only half real, should want to feed him and touch him because he also had pale hair.

They stayed at Zuni only a day and pushed on into the high White Mountains. Cold winds blew here at night and even the days were chilly. The ridges bore yellow pine, often a hundred feet high, making an open forest of warm red columns and dark green crowns that patterned the needle-shiny earth with shadow. Wild turkeys, sometimes in bunches of a hundred, ran away among trees or rose with a roar like a storm and sailed on set wings across sharp-cut gorges. Great silver-gray squirrels with white bellies and black-tasselled ears loped gracefully over the ground and up the trees. Except when wild things moved or cried this forest held a hush that seemed to shut the mouths of men.

As they went farther they rode nervously. Fresh pony tracks were in the trail and they found recent ashes of small Indian fires. Apaches were at peace but nobody trusted Apaches.

A tall Mexican named Santestevan had been elected captain but Tom Foote became the real leader now because he knew Indians.

"They've spotted us," he told Robert. "You can

[73]

bet they're watching us all the time. If they're gonna act right they ought to send somebody to lead us in. . . ."

All rode uneasily, feeling unseen Indian eyes, until one morning three naked brown men came riding to meet them, held up flat hands in sign of friendship, and became their guides.

They first saw the Apache camp from a hill top. It was in a flat green valley walled close with pine and rock. Round yellow-thatched Apache huts, scattered in three groups, looked like little haystacks from above and they could see figures moving and a great herd of horses and mules in the lower valley with mounted men on guard.

Their guides put hands to mouths and gave yodelling yells. Out of the valley came a chorus of answer from a hundred at once with dogs joining in. Blankets waved and figures ran and multiplied. They rode down and sat their horses still but anxious while Apaches swarmed around them in a pushing grunting mob of lean brown dirty men in breech clouts and knee-high Apache boot moccasins, and squat short-skirted women, naked to the waist, with long scraggly pendulous breasts and snakey black hair hanging over peering eyes.

The crowd broke to let through a tall Indian, walking erect and proud. Tom Foote and Santestevan got off their horses to meet him. He was a man of beautiful build, deep-chested and big-

muscled, but smooth as a woman, not bunchy like
a nervous hard-working white man. He was naked
as the others but his face was painted with scarlet
and ochre in spots and circles and three fine eagle
feathers waved in his hair. He was smeared all
over with some kind of grease that made him glis-
ten in the sun and look bigger and it stank like
rancid lard. In his right hand he carried a lance
about eight feet long with a black jagged obsidian
point. As he came forward he stooped suddenly
and laid his weapon on the ground. He stretched
out a hand, its finger nails half an inch long and
caked black with dirt.

"I am Cochise, the whiteman's friend," he said
in Spanish. *"Da me* tobacco."

When he had been given presents he led them to
huts and told them whatever they left there would
be safe.

"Apaches are not thieves like Navajos," he said.

They were guests now and protected. The Mexicans cautiously stuck to their quarters but Tom
and Robert wandered around the huge camp all
evening to stare and be stared at.

A boy of about twenty joined them who looked
just like an apache in every way except that he was
a little lighter and had greenish eyes. He told them
he came from Sonora and had been captured by
the Apaches when he was nine years old. He didn't
want to be bought and taken home as Tom at first

thought. "I am Apache!" he told them. "I spit on Mexicans!" He spit on an imaginary Mexican as he said it. What he wanted was a job as interpreter for next day's trading.

They saw that luck was with them. The Indians had far more mules and horses than they could winter. They were killing mules to eat every day. Tom and Robert saw them peg down a young mule and skin his quivering hind quarters while he was alive and groaning. They liked the meat better that way. After they had carved living steaks to the bone they cut the mule's throat and mothers tenderly gave little children hot blood to drink.

Late in the day a party of eight young men rode in driving thirty or forty more mules they had stolen in Mexico. A mob gathered around them and they showed two scalpes, one of a woman with brown hair a yard long, and all shouted and grunted when these were held up. About sunset a scalp dance started and the visitors, from a little way off, saw women chanting and swaying around kettles of stewing mule meat, saw the scalp pole passed around for everyone to spit on, heard proud young warriors tell their tales of blood.

Old women with shrivelled breasts and ragged gray hair, hopping and shuffling round a fire in a slow thumping measure, spitting on hair torn off murdered heads, held Robert in staring fascinated horror. . . .

[76]

"Come on, let's turn in," said Tom. "Them old wenches'll caper all night."

The hut they lived in was made by bending planted poles and tying them at the top. The walls were of hides, mostly horse and mule, and the roof was a thick thatch of coarse yellow grass. It was clean inside.

Just as they were turning in, a little man came to the door wearing a tattered cotton shirt and dirty buckskin trousers. He was barefooted and had long hair and a thick short beard both turning gray. In good Spanish, in a voice that was a weak and humble quaver, he asked for tobacco. He too was a captive and had been one for five years.

He sat before the hut a long while and talked a little. When he was not talking he sang in a very small voice a song which had for its refrain, *"O sonora, mi hierra!"* His singing was a wail of pure anguish without hope. Tom asked him why he didn't run away and he said he was afraid. But neither did he want to be bought. . . . They finally got it out of him that he did not want to go back, that he could never face his own people again because of something the Indians had done to him when he was first captured. . . .

"I am dead," he told them, "Although I walk around . . ." He wept a little. They finally sent him away with much tobacco and a comb and heard him in the dark still singing, "O beautiful Sonora."

[77]

Next day Robert sorted out merchandise and kept tab while Tom Foote, red-faced, perspiring, alert and intense, traded for mules and horses. Each animal he examined with a few swift sure gestures, forcing its mouth open, running a hand down each leg, scanning back and belly for galls and sores. He refused everything over six years old. For each animal he made his offer, and then, without waiting for a reply, directed Robert to pile up the goods and left the Indian to think. He knew he could buy at his own price and he refused to haggle. Under his brusque half-angry manner visibly bubbled a great elation.

"We didn't cross all them mountains fer nothin'," pardner," he remarked to Robert once. "If only it don't snow on us now, this here is a clean-up!"

Chapter Ten

DRIVING a drumming dusty herd before them they took the home trail and pushed the stock hard.

Tom Foote now was a silent worried general. He kept everything moving, rode ahead to pick the best grass and water, rode behind to watch the back track in case some young buck should take a notion to follow and steal. At night he posted guards to watch the herd and watched it most of the time himself. He said almost nothing except to throw an occasional thunderous Goddam at a lagging mule. He ate little and slept little and seemed angry all the time. He radiated a ferocious nervous energy that kept men and horses on the jump.

They were near the top of the divide when the sky turned a solid dirty purple-gray like the skin of a man seven days drowned. Tom Foote lifted a face of rage to heaven.

"God damn the Goddam weather!" he pronounced solemnly.

"Chiguela Chingado cabron!" chanted Miguel Romero.

They pushed on in a silent rage while great

white flakes came down and touched their faces gently.

White flakes thickened so that when they topped the ridge they could not see a hundred feet. . . . They rode on a lost fragment of the earth wandering in empty whiteness of infinite storm.

In tall pine forests the snow piled deep and slowed their going. The feet of shod horses balled so that they slipped and floundered.

When the snow let up for a while late in the afternoon it was already a foot deep and the sky promised more.

Snow hung beautifully on high pines and made sweetly modelled mounds of scrub oak thickets. The wind went down. Not a wild thing moved. The earth had turned white and died and lay beautiful but useless. When they camped the mules and horses pawed futilely for buried grass and they scraped away snow to make beds and dug under snow for wood.

It snowed off and on for three days and then it turned cold and rained and after that it snowed some more. Starving mules and horses shrank and bulged their ribs, weakened, stumbled and fell. All were afoot now for horses couldn't carry them. Robert's boots began to wear out and he walked on wet and blistered feet.

They went only half as far as they should have gone in a day. They killed no game and grub ran low. When a pack horse fell and broke a leg he was skinned and butchered and they chewed boiled horse. They were out of salt except for some cakes of salty whitish earth the Apaches had given them.

Robert chewed and swallowed gritty boiled horse and held it down with an effort. In the long rain he slept sitting up most of the time and waked so stiff and cramped he thought he would never move again. Toward the end of each day he felt he could go only another hundred yards. He would fix his eyes on a tree or a rock a little way ahead and swear to reach it, and when he did he would pick out another goal and try again. He lived from minute to minute, from rock to rock. He had no thought but to keep going, no desire but to live . . . not to go down under rolling blowing snow where everything was dead, not to go down into buried frozen earth . . . only to stay on top and struggle, only to live and see the sun!

They hadn't seen the sun in five days. They began to realize they were lost when Tom Foote and Santestevan got into an argument about which way was east. They differed by ninety degrees and each was sure he knew. They almost fought and finally flipped a coin to decide. Santestevan won, and he led them up on a great flat mesa where pines towered over them and dead level lay all around. There was no hill to climb, no visible drainage to follow.

[81]

They slowed and stopped in a huddle of beaten
men and beasts. Horses and mules stood with tails
to a cold wind that ruffled long ragged hair over
gaunt ribs. Three horses lay down and everybody
knew they would never get up.

Robert sat down on a rock. "This is probably
where I die," he thought wearily. But still he hoped
not. Tom Foote looked at him and smiled a gaunt
smile.

"Tough titty, old man!" he remarked. "Don't
you wisht you was back home with your little warm
muchacha?"

About a hundred yards away was a high green
pine with a dead one leaning against it, so a man
might with much labor climb up to the first sound
limbs and so to the top. Santestevan wanted someone to climb that tree. He thought they were nearly out of the mountains and from a height one
might see the flats and learn which way to go.

Tom listened to him in disgust.

"Climb it yourself, you poor goddam misguided
fool!" he suggested.

Santestevan tried but he was a clumsy heavy
man and fell off the dead tree before he reached
the live one.

Robert rose and walked toward the tree feebly.
He had climbed many trees years ago to get nuts.
He knew he could climb that tree and he knew

he had to do it. They watched him wearily, full of doubt.

It was easy enough after he got to the big tree. It was just like a ladder. And the earth opened out vast before him as he rose. He saw flat lands, not many miles away. They looked purple, with scanty patches of white.

When he was nearly down he slipped off the dead tree and fell. Santestevan ran to him, pulled him up and shouted in his ear.

"What did you see, what did you see?"

He seemed afraid Robert might die before he gave the news.

Robert waved a hand and pointed.

"That way," he said. "No snow . . . hardly any snow . . ."

He began to rub his head with snow and feel his joints. He was all right.

Now for the first time he took the lead. Everyone picked up sudden energy.

Horses dying in the snow lifted sad eyes, made a last struggle to rise, fell back and gave it up.

Down on the flats, snow was skimpy and wind had brushed it off the high spots. Famished animals began tearing at short yellow grass. It was hard to hold them till packs and saddles were off.

As soon as the stock was loose the Mexicans began foraging among low scrubby pinon trees like hungry squirrels. Smashing open cones with

rocks they got out little meaty nuts. Tom and
Robert followed suit. Miguel Romero, with a
yell of pure joy, unearthed a pack-rat's nest that
held a peck of nuts stored for winter. All plunged
hands in and crammed mouths, chewed nuts shell
and all, laughing and eager. . . . They had eaten
nothing but meat for eighteen days.

Chapter Eleven

WHEN they got back to the valley it was near Christmas. Ice floated in the river and gleamed blue on the lagoons that spotted brown pasture lands. Cottonwoods were naked gray. Snow-covered mountains rose in sharp white angles and flying wildfowl wrote black streaming figures on the cold pale sky.

The valley roads were full of travel for this was a time of much visiting, when great families gathered. Young horsemen in new suits and hats galloped by with a shout and a wave of the hand. The poor rolled by in noisy wagon-loads and they saw several great coaches of the rich with women and children peering out and men riding alongside on fine horses. There would be now grand balls in the halls of great houses and humble public dances in every plaza. It was a time of wine and love. The lean travelers rode eagerly.

When they clattered into the plaza people crowded about them shaking hands and asking questions. Even old Doxey, who had been grumpy when they left, came out to congratulate them and offered to take most of their mules off their hands at a fair price. Young Diego embraced them both and said that life had been dull without his two best amigos and announced that he was taking them both to his house where all of his many cousins, uncles and aunts were gathered for the holidays.

He led Robert aside and told him laughing:

"Your little sweetheart is gone. She married a man from Socorro about a month after you left. . . . She was too lonely without you."

He seemed to think it a fine joke but when he saw the disappointed look in Robert's face he slapped him on the back.

"Never mind, Amigo," he said. "There are so many women in the world!"

Robert forgot all about his loss for a moment when he went into a room at Tolliver's and looked at his own face in a mirror for the first time in over three months. He saw a man with hair that hung down on his neck and thick whiskers embroidering a brick-red face. His eyes were bright with health and narrowed from long staring into the glare of snow and desert. Hardly anything about his own face was familiar. He felt with a shock that he looked at another. . . . After careful consideration he decided to keep his beard.

As soon as he entered the sala of the Aragons he realized that he was a new man to others as well as to himself. The great room was banked with unfamiliar faces, but all of the family were there—even Nina, home on a visit—and all of them came forward and embraced him. He was an old friend of the family now, returned from perilous adventures. He was no longer an alien but a man tried and proved in the ways of the country.

Only Nina hung back from the embrace of welcome. When he turned toward her she tossed her head and laughed and he paused, embarrassed. . . . It was not the same Nina. She was not shy now but coquettish. The limpid virginal look was gone. Her eyes danced and hid.

"Go on!" her mother encouraged. "Give your amigo a kiss. . . . When he has been gone so long! Wild Indians might have killed him!"

Nina came forward, laughing still, and gave him a cheek to kiss. Then, under pretense of struggle, she swiftly touched his mouth with hers, briefly thrust a meaning tongue between his lips. It was a touch as light and quick as the fall of a rain drop and it rocked him on his heels like a heavy blow.

He had been so long away from women that he had forgotten how they looked, how they tasted. Never before had they struck so sharply upon his every sense. The touch of their hands and arms, so inconceivably soft and delicate, the mysterious bulge of their bosoms, the faint sweet odor of their hair—all made his blood pound. He felt as though he breathed a strangely stimulating air. . . . If he had not gone on a long trip into a world of savages, snow and starvation he would never have known what strange disturbing creatures women were.

He sat in the hot red room cluttered with skirts and curtains, holding a little red shell of wine in stiff and calloused fingers. He felt large awkward and strong, more than equal to this warmed and sheltered world, a little out of place in it. He was eager, he was glad but yet he sat unconcerned as never before. Some over-anxious twittering part of himself he had left behind in a waste of snow where life shrank to a moment of pain and struggle.

He looked with curiosity at all these rich Mexicans—the women dressed in spreading velvets, with hair piled over high combs and heavy golden jewelry set with emeralds and rubies on their necks and hands and arms. Old Dona Alarid, who had come all the way from El Paso to visit her married daughter, sat like an ancient shrivelled queen in a high-backed arm chair and used for a footstool an Indian servant who lay on the floor.

Robert was amused by all he saw but his restless eyes kept hunting the eyes of Nina, catching them once in a while for an enigmatic instant. . . . Her look filled him with wonder and with a tremble of hope he tried to deny.

They had an immense supper with wild turkeys, ducks and a whole roasted suckling pig, with wine and grape brandy to top it and for dessert a fragrant Mexican confection made by roasting sprouted grain in an adobe oven. Afterward they played all the old games in a boisterous roar.

Don Aragon led Robert solemnly into another room and asked for an exact account of all he had done. Had he made money on his trip and what were his plans?

Robert told him they had brought through more than half of their horses and mules alive. They had made a profit, they would buy wagons—but their start as overland freighters would have to be a small one.

The Don tapped him on the chest with a finger.

"I will give you a credit of three thousand dollars in St. Louis," he announced. He waved his hand with a gesture of easy largess when Robert started to say his thanks. "No, No! The money will be well placed. I bet on you as I would bet on a horse when I have seen him run."

Robert came out of the house a little dazed by so much luck and hospitality, by so many ponies of white brandy, but when he took off his hat and let the cold December wind blow on his brow he felt as though his every vein and muscle bulged with life.

He was walking homeward slowly when he heard a step behind him and turned. The small bent figure of an old peon woman with a serape cowled over head and shoulders hurried after him. When she came up he recognized her as a woman who had worked about the Aragon place ever since he had first gone there, whom he had often served in the store.

"Senor Roberto," she said, "you must come back to the house in about an hour. Come to the little gate at the back and knock there. . . . Dona Nina sent me!"

She gave him a shrivelled smile and hurried back the way she had come, leaning against the wind.

Robert spent his hour prowling restlessly in the dark, afraid that if he went to the hotel he would get into some conversation hard to leave. He kept thinking of Nina's kiss and the teasing look in her eyes, refusing to let himself believe that what he hoped was true.

The whole of the Aragon house was black and still when he came to the little gate. His hand trembled with eagerness when he lifted it to knock. The old woman opened the gate almost immediately, as though she had been waiting there, and without a word she led him across the placita. The doors of almost all the rooms opened upon it. She stopped at one of these and instead of knocking, scratched with a finger nail. There was about the whole thing an air of intrigue profoundly secretive and carefully planned.

The door opened and closed behind him and he

[90]

stood in pitch dark, bewildered. Then he heard a
laugh he knew. It was a laugh full of mischief and
challenge with something hard and ruthless in it
too—the laugh of a woman traded and used,
watched and guarded, taking her sweet revenge
on all her masters. . . . He felt bare arms about
his neck and a mouth upon his own. . . .

The night was almost gone when he came out
and started again for Tolliver's. The sky was getting pale in the East, roosters were crowing and it
was intensely cold. But he was warmed through
and through. He felt a mild elation, a deep gratitude, a peacefulness that reached out and caressed everything. He was glad he had starved
and frozen and gone unloved so long because that
made it so much the sweeter to be rocked in the
warm white cradle of a tender vagrant lust. Never
before had the sweetness of life so filled his mouth,
the moment so completely answered to the mood.

When he got back to his cold room he lit a
candle and looked joyfully at cracked walls and a
ragged bed. Remembering his one other night in
that hotel he spread his blankets on the floor. He
was unused to mattresses anyway. . . . Then his
eyes fell on a packet of mail for him lying on the
table. He had forgotten all about mail. . . . He
cut the string and saw the handwriting on many
letters, feeling his spirits sink like something cold
and heavy sliding down his throat and hitting the

pit of his stomach. Most of the letters were from Elizabeth. With a wrinkled brow he sat until dawn reading them—all about her devotion unchanging and God knows best and the wonderful days they had had together. . . . Surely this was not real. . . . Surely this was a book he read about two foolish lovers long ago.

Over finely penned letters he sat long puzzled. He thought of a reply—that he was no longer the boy who had gone away and promised—and knew he would never write it. The memory of New England, of golden hair and Annie Laurie, of white houses along a shady street, seemed remote and static like a picture on a wall. It seemed no part of life at all. And yet he was bound to it by ties too deep understand, too strong to break.

His love of Elizabeth was a memory but her fidelity was a fact. It was a link in his destiny that he could not break.

Reluctantly he knew he would go back when he could.

SECOND PART

INDIANS

Chapter One

IN those days when the Union Pacific was pushing West, when gold in the Black Hills started another rush, when hide hunters were wiping out the buffalo, the prairie and mountain Indians began to go bad.

Government made treaties and broke them, settlers swarmed over Indian lands, agents and traders cheated and lied, white men planted syphilis in red women and poured liquor into red men.

All the Indians that rode horses and hunted buffalo began painting their faces black and fighting for revenge. They saw their day was over. They thought their Gods were angry. They hated white men now as they had never hated before.

Gone were the days of little horse-stealing parties playing hide-and-seek with trappers and hunters, days of bow-and-arrow Indians, who fought without plan. Indians now had Winchesters, six shooters and field glasses. They rode a thousand strong and more and they had leaders that outfoxed and out-fought the army. Those were the days of Crazy Horse, Sitting Bull, Geronimo, Little Crow, Chief Joseph and Washakie.

In those days ranches and mines were working

all along the foot of the mountains and up into the mountain valleys from Montana to Arizona. Men had been living there safe and busy for years.

All the great trails fror Oregon to Texas carried steady travel and trade with just a scare or a murder now and then.

All at once Indians struck ranches, mines and wagon trains.

Those were the days of surprises and outrages that filled the papers, of lurid stories written by reporters who followed Crook and Custer, of Indian controversy between Easterners who loved Indians because they had been wronged, and Westerners who hated Indians because they had killed wives and children and burned crops and houses.

The Sioux in the North went on a rampage and killed seven hundred. The troops that followed them found whole settlements dead, starving pigs and dogs eating rotten human bodies, stench of death filling every house. They found a woman dead by a stove and her baby baked in the oven along with a cake. They found eleven children dead in a wagon and one spiked to a fence post with a wagon bolt. They hunted Indians, killed a few, made another treaty. Thirty-eight Indians they hanged for murder. The Indians shook hands all around, smiled, sang and died happy.

In Colorado the Arapahoes, Cheyenne and Kiowa killed hundreds, stopped all stage lines and wagon trains that fed the country, burned crops, left mountain settlements starving. Flour went up to forty-five dollars a barrel. The governor of Colorado wired to Washington for help and none came. Colorado Volunteers surprised an Indian village, shot down squaws along with bucks, shot down Indian children running for the brush. "Nits make lice," they said.

Down in the hot South Apaches had had everything their own way for two hundred years, raided and traded to suit themselves. Now two governments put troops on their trail. The Mexicans offered a bounty for Apache scalps. An American miner invited a band of Apaches to eat, shot down the feasting Indians with a little swivel cannon like a bunch of ducks on a sandbar, collected his money on their hair.

Mangus Colorado, great Apache chief, came in under a flag of truce to talk. They killed him and cut off his head and sent it to Washington. Scientists said his brain was bigger than Daniel Webster's and settlers said: "There's one brown bastard won't do us no more dirt."

In those days a world was being destroyed—an old and savage world, rich in Gods and rituals, a world of cruel happy children living in a fairyland of imagined monsters. . . . A wild beautiful world was being destroyed with engines and guns, with germs and poisons, by an invader who ravaged the women as he ravaged the earth and polluted the blood as he fouled the water. . . . Against him flamed a violence that was hot, short and sudden, like grass fire before a wind.

Those were the days of men burned alive, of ears and noses cut off living faces, of women pegged down and raped and babies tossed in the air and caught on the points of Apache lances.

After every raid and battle yelling squaws came running with their knives to strip and mutilate the dead, waving bloody trophies, to cut off hands and feet and gouge out eyes that ghosts of white men might go maimed and impotent to meet their Gods.

Chapter Two

THE wagon train of Jayson and Foote, merchant freighters, traveled slowly along the valley of the Arkansas between Walnut Creek and Pawnee Rock.

It was late August. Blooming sunflowers shoulder high to a man on horseback lined a white road deep in sand. The river was low and made a curving silver scar on the white glaring face of its sandy flood plain. Round low sandhills beyond were bare except for a few aged and stunted cottonwoods that grew high enough to escape floods but too high to get much water. They made blots of deep shadow on bald pale slopes under the crooked shimmer of the heat—the dry cloudless maddening heat of the prairie. No living thing moved in it but men and their mules and the sunloving insects that sing and buzz and seem to give the heat a voice. Everything else lay down in shade and waited, but men never wait and insects sting them on their restless way.

Five wagons, loaded high and sheeted white, each pulled by six fly-tortured mules, lifted a thin pale screen of dust that hung in the air for a mile behind. Jim Arvis, wagon master, drove the front wagon. Hunched in his seat, he spat long squirts of brown tobacco juice and picked large gray horse-flies off twitching mule-rumps with a practiced lash.

A light spring wagon, called an ambulance, with two seats and a white top, followed the leader. Elizabeth, Robert's bride, rode in the back seat. The wide spread of her bright blue dress showed like a banner in the sun and the little fringed para-sol she tilted against it seemed a futile imperti-nence. Her leather trunk was strapped on behind and from a top strut hung a wooden cage where an unhappy canary bird fluttered on his rocking perch.

Robert rode a tall bay Kentucky saddle mule of great power and bottom. The mule was restless under the sting of horseflies and Robert was anx-ious, although he kept telling himself there was nothing to worry about. He did not believe in danger from Indians or from anything else. He had made this trip five times with no greater ca-tastrophe than one wagon lost in the quicksands of the Cimarron crossing. But he was painfully aware of Elizabeth, fragile and worried, rocking uncom-fortably in her seat. He would be glad when they got out of the valley where the sunflowers grew so thick and tall.

He rode restlessly up and down the train pre-tending to watch for hot-boxes and collar-galls but really too nervous to keep the crawling pace of his wagons. As he passed Elizabeth from the front she smiled at him bravely, brushing a wisp of hair away from her eyes. But when he rode up from behind he could see the rigid suffering in the line of her back. Her hand gripped the edge of a seat so that her knuckles paled and her thin cheek quivered to the shock of wheels hitting rock and rut. She didn't know how to relax and roll with the sway and bump of the carriage. In fact it seemed to him she had never relaxed a waking moment since they left St. Louis. The whole journey had been a torture to her. At night mosquitoes filled her tent and the sun burned and sickened her all day. The motion of the carriage gave her nausea and so did the sight of a mule with a gaping festered sore on its neck, and a rattlesnake crushed by a wheel and writhing in the road made her shriek with horror. . . . But worse than anything that happened was her dread of what might—a dread that showed in her eyes, that held her tense, that she could neither hide nor explain.

They camped at Pawnee Rock and Jim Arvis came to help Robert put up her tent and make her as comfortable as possible. Jim was a short powerful bowlegged man with a dirty tangle of red hair and red whiskers stained with tobacco juice. His face was a brighter shade, despite the dirt, and the cross-hatching of wrinkles in the ruddy leather of his neck was filled with grime like ore in the rock. He treated Elizabeth with a chivalry that was worship, taking off his hat and disgorging his chew before he came near, but Elizabeth could not see beyond his dirt. Robert had asked him to eat with them once, and then no more, for both of them suffered.

Elizabeth ate little this evening and retired at once, closing the tent flap. She was always eager to be in the tent and reluctant to leave it, glad of anything with four walls to shut out a great barren terrifying world.

Robert and Arvis sat over tin coffee cups talking about waterholes, grass and Indians. Their Indian scare was based on little—mostly on the fact they had seen no Indians. When Indians came into camp to beg and talk they were surely friendly and when they didn't show at all you didn't know.

On every trip before Robert had met the Comanchee chief, White Buffalo and his little band and he and the chief were friends of a sort. White Buffalo always put on his blue military coat with gold shoulder straps and his plug hat when he came to camp. That was all he wore except a gee-string. Robert had given him pants but he couldn't stand them. They made his legs itch. He had an enormous capacity for beans which he crammed into his mouth by the handful. He had told Robert more than once that they were brothers.

Brother White Buffalo hadn't appeared this trip. One smoke signal a long way off they had seen, and pony tracks of a small band crossing the road just before they got to Fort Yarah on the little Arkansas where one company of cavalry was camped. Robert asked them for an escort and they told him he didn't need one, there was no danger. If he was scared he could wait till more wagons came along. He wasn't scared so he went on.

He didn't like the military. None of the wagon people did. They thought the soldiers only made the Indians worse. Before the government began building army posts and patrolling the road they never had any trouble. . . . On the way east he had met the big expedition that went north looking for the Sioux, with infantry and cavalry both and mountain howitzers packed on mules. A young officer came to camp to "talk Indian" with him— a handsome young man with long yellow hair and yellow whiskers. He looked like something dressed up to play a part but they said he was a gifted Indian fighter who went crazy in battle and fought like a maniac without ever losing his skill. This man, Robert saw, fought Indians for the love of it. He loved the battles he had known and he lusted for more battles. His great ambition was to corner a band of Sioux and hit them with a full-company cavalry charge—a thing that had never been done. He was having a good time but unless he killed all the Indians he wouldn't make travel any safer.

[103]

After he had eaten and talked enough to feel easy Robert went to the tent to see Elizabeth. He found her dressed in some flouncey white thing sitting up on her cot with her feet tucked under and slim white arms embracing her knees, while wide and worried eyes searched the floor.

"O Robert, I'm so glad you came. . . . Something fell off the roof and hit my face, some horrible crawley thing. . . . Didn't you hear me scream? It fell on the floor and I can't see it and I can't bear to have it in here. It makes me think of that snake."

Robert searched the ground, discovered a long-legged harmless spider and crushed it under his foot.

"It's dead now, dear," he said patiently.

He sat down beside her, took her hand and began to stroke her hair. He was not making love to a woman, he was comforting a frightened child. She leaned against him wearily and he kissed her on unresisting unresponding lips.

Out of tenderness desire slowly grew. He imagined in her what he felt in himself. It seemed as though a long-lost moment was coming back. . . .

"O Elizabeth!" His arms claimed her, his lips pushed her head back.

Instantly she stiffened against him. There was no yield in her, no answer. She was like a frightened kitten putting out involuntary claws, not to hurt but to save itself from some uncomprehended disaster.

He let her go and sat back looking at her with weary puzzled hopeless eyes. She met his look a moment, blinking at her tears, then buried her face against him, clutched his shirt with thin nervous hands that needed to cling but could not give. The vibration of her sobbing went clear through him, filled him with her pain.

"O Robert, I can't help it, I can't help it! I waited too long. If only you had taken me with you when first you went! I'm not the same any more and neither are you. I waited too long!"

Pity killed desire. Pity shrank and weakened him. He sat silent, the inert recipient of her misery, knowing pity bound him as desire never could.

Suddenly she flung back her head and spread her arms with a gesture more of despair than of invitation.

"Take me, Robert!" she cried. "Take me! I'm no good but I'm yours. Take me!"

He kissed her on the cheek and patted her shoulder.

"Not now, dear," he said. "It'll be different when we get there. You're tired and frightened now."

He made her lie down and covered her up.

"I'll sit by you till you go to sleep and I won't

let anything bite you either. Now you must go to sleep. It'll be different when we get there."

Sleep at last unclenched her hands and gently rocked her bosom.

Robert lit a lantern and hung it on the tent pole. She wanted light all the time.

He went out into cool evening and walked away from camp toward the high shelving rock that gave the place its name.

The first time he ever camped there he had climbed that rock and spent half of a moonlight night on top of it. He remembered that night as one that had marked a change and made a difference. Always before he had been more than half afraid of the long road he was destined to travel over and over. He had often felt lost in the blaze of the prairie day, in the black of the prairie night. He had longed for a smaller safer more settled world.

That night he had discovered, as though by revelation that he loved the wilderness.

In peace and pleasure he had looked out over evening-shadowed prairie studded to the horizon with grazing buffalo. He took half a continent for his dooryard and was glad he lived in nothing smaller. The sandhills to the north curtained a mystery and he was glad it was there.

He sat that night till the sun went down and the moon came up, till coyotes sang and were silent, till the last fire in his own camp died and the world became limitless with a dim uncertain beauty that hid a thousand dangers. But still he liked it and was not afraid. He sat until nearly midnight blowing the smoke of his pipe at the stars, cocking his feet in the face of the moon, feeling as much a piece of the earth as the rock on which he sat.

Since then he had climbed the rock every time he camped there. He had never again caught quite the same mood. That was like the first kiss of a love, a thrill that never repeated. But he had always found peace there and a touch of unaccountable happiness.

He did not find either this night. The sky was fair, the shadow-rumpled prairie was beautiful and the river was fallen fire in the last light of the sun. But he was small and afraid, no longer a fit companion for moons and mountains—no more than she was. For she had become a part of him and he shared her dread and her misery. . . .

Like strangers they had met in St. Louis, looking at each other with a surprise that neither could hide. He did not know how much she had really changed in those years but she was so much thinner and wispier than he had thought. And he was heavier, burned and bearded. She did not know him at first.

Their marriage so far had been a frustrate

misery, with Elizabeth ill and frightened, and yet her hold upon him had grown day by day. It had become the business of his life to get her safely home and make her somehow happy. But could it be done? Five years of her youth she had spent in the old white house, embroidering flowers on linen, drinking tea with old ladies and praying to God. He had doomed her to that and now he dragged her frightened and sick into a wilderness. . . . The night for him was filled with doubt and guilt.

Back to the camp he went without ever getting away from her for a minute, and stood looking at her asleep before he lay down himself. Her lips were a little open, her arms crossed the blanket, her breasts lifted lightly against the covering.

He felt ashamed and tender as he looked at her asleep. Her unconscious mouth was so childlike. . . . Her breasts were buds that had never known warmth enough to swell.

Once she had been all women to him but now she lay in his mind beside other women—one tawny and strong with a neck like a tree who took her man as a willing beast takes a burden, as the earth takes a plow . . . and another slim and satin-soft with generations of artful adultery behind her, whose lips and hands made music in the blood.

He remembered without caring. Elizabeth came long before either, belonged to an older part of himself. They had set him free by meeting his desire. She bound him by the pain that bound him to the past.

He did not despise her weakness because he had shared it. Her fear of wilderness and night, of love and blood, had been his own. And underneath her weakness lay the steel of her hard New England strength. She was frightened and yet she refused her own fear. A spider could make her scream but she never spoke of going back. Wilderness filled her with a sense of doom and she went to meet it.

Moreover, her very weakness seemed to answer to his need. She was his discipline, his lone long fidelity, and he yearned to make his destiny hers. He had learned to live by living and he would teach her. He had learned to love and he would bring her the wisdom of his sins. In her he would plant the seeds of his lust and they would flower in tenderness. . . . One throb of response from her would be worth more than a dozen easy surrenders. . . . Money he had gathered and she was the use for it. He had built her a house with a board floor, blue china and a harp for her to play. . . . Through her he would bring the past into the present and bridge the gulf that sundered him from home and an older self . . .

Chapter Three

LULLED by the sun and by the roll and jog of
their going they were all sleepy and dull by
late afternoon. Mules moved slowly and no whips
cracked. The deep sand of the road muffled noise
as it killed speed. All looked forward to camp and
cool water and considered another day already
over.

Robert rode beside the train, slouching and nodding in his saddle. Without interest he saw Arvis
stand up in his wagon and look. Arvis was picking
a place to camp. That was a part of his job. Then
he saw the man point and heard a shout that shattered the dull moment.

"By God. . . . There they are!"

He wheeled his mule and rode between wagons.
Nearly two hundred yards away, just coming over
a rise among tall sunflowers, he saw a few horsemen—eight or ten. He saw one more clearly on a
tall gray horse, saw feathers in a savage head, the
glint of sun on a gun barrel. . . . He dropped
off his restless mule and dragged his rifle from its
scabbard.

The Indian on the gray horse stopped and raised
an arm in signal. Over the rise came riding more,

massing behind a leader. Then, all at once, in a move as perfectly timed as the wheeling of wild-fowl in the air, they shot forward lashing and yell-ing, some waving blankets to stampede the mules, some low on their horses to shoot.

He shot at the gray horse and saw it plunge and the white glint of its belly when it rolled.

As though the shot had broken their ranks, they divided, one part rushing at the head of the train to turn it, while the other struck for the rear.

Their charge split a minute. It was only a flash and a yell answered by a crack of rifles and whips and a shout at mules. . . . He stood in thick dust jamming a fresh brass cartridge into the breech of his gun. He ran between wagons and saw dimly one wagon and the ambulance going across the valley in a dead run, surrounded by yelling horse-men who had mules by the bridles and lashed them with rope-ends. . . . Above the din he heard a thin high scream of pure terror. . . .

That scream drove him wholly mad. He shot wildly into dust, reloaded and ran after. . . . From behind someone caught him. He heard the voice of one of his Mexicans telling him to come back. He saw a bullet throw up a spurt of earth at his feet and heard the whine of its ricochet. He was thrown on his face and held. Two men dragged him back to the wagons.

Arvis had kept his mules to the road and so

saved the whole train from stampede, but the flanking party had killed one driver and turned one wagon and the ambulance.

The other wagons were already forted in a circle with men lying flat between wheels and popping at a dust cloud, and frightened mules backing and snorting in a tangle of harness.

A quarter of a mile away the dust cloud came to a stop in an arroyo that hid all but a wagon-top and heads of horsemen. Whether the Indians had stopped on purpose or stalled in deep sand it was hard to say. Anyway, they were out of range.

Robert got up and started around to where Arvis lay. A bullet smashed the tailboard of a wagon beside him. The Indians had thrown out a picket line and were trying to find the range. A Mexican boy about eighteen years old, who helped wrangle the mules, jumped up and tried to pull Robert down. Robert turned and hit him with his fist, saw and only half noticed the blood well out of his lips and the look of amazement in the boy's eyes. . . . He bent over Arvis and grabbed him by the shoulder.

"Come on!" he shouted. "We can't lie here and let 'em kill her. God knows what they'll do. . . . Come on!"

Arvis rolled up sitting and gripped Robert's arm in a great stubby hand.

"You're crazy, man! You're plumb crazy!

There's six of us and more'n a hundred of them. We wouldn't get fifty feet from the wagons. We'd just give 'em the outfit. You gotta lay down and take it, same as the rest of us. We're lucky if we stand 'em off. I know it's hell, but you gotta lay down and take it. . . ."

Chapter Four

In front rode a full company of dragoons—men
in blue coats and weathered gray campaign hats
pulled low, mounted on heavy fat grainfed bay
horses under full equipment of blanket roll, ration,
canteen and carbine. They rode at ease, talking
and chewing tobacco, some excited by the hope of
battle, some grumbling and mopping sweat like
hands in a cornfield. A spectacular young officer
with long yellow hair and drooping yellow moustache rode beside a shabby old man on a tall single-
footing gray mule, with a long sharp's rifle across
the front of his saddle. This was Stillwell, the scout,
who was supposed to lead the soldiers to Indians
as a guide leads sportsmen to game.

Behind the dragoons came four mules packed
with mountain howitzers and another young officer was in charge of these and of the gunners.
Behind the guns twenty Ute trailers rode their
scrawney patchwork of many-colored ponies. They
were naked to the waist, with dirty blankets
bunched around their middles. Most of them had
black paint on their faces and the sun glinted on
the greasy black of their hair. A few squaws followed with pack ponies. The Indians joked and

laughed. This was a picnic to them. They were paid to trail and fight Comanchees they hated.

Behind the Indians rode five civilians. All of these had lost mules and merchandise to the Comanchees, and one of them, Robert Jayson, had lost a wife. They had all applied at Fort Learned for military escorts to go out and hunt what they had lost. Each had expected to get maybe a squad, none had hoped for much success. Meantime scouts had come in and reported two Indian villages on the little Arkansas. The raiding Indians had feinted a trail south, split up, regathered, and gone north. Bad Indians, stolen goods and prisoners, if any lived, were almost surely in the great camp on the little Arkansas. Comanchee, Kiowa and Apache were banded together there. Now was the time to smash them. . . . The military escorts requested by wronged civilians had combined and grown into an expedition. The civilians, almost forgotten, were allowed to trail along.

The troop would move all day and part of the night with scouts fanned out before it. With luck it would camp three miles from Indians who thought they were safe. With luck troops would shoot into sleeping tepees at dawn. . . .

Robert had slept little in four nights. The night after the raid they lay under their wagons till two in the morning. They saw the Indians send up huge signal flares made by setting barrels of whisky on fire. Then the stolen wagon and the ambulance were burned and they saw moving shapes against a red glare. When the fires died down they crawled out in the dark and found only embers and twisted red hot iron. After that they made the drive to Learned.

Robert now rode silent except that once in a while he found himself talking to Elizabeth. The others who rode with him believed he was crazy, what with the heat and all this trouble, and they treated him with worried kindness. A little sandy-haired fellow named Gilchrist had his head full of Indian. He was nervous and wanted to talk. He started telling about what Indians did to women and Maguffey shut him up short, jerking a thumb at Robert. Maguffey was a heavy red-faced man with a great black moustache who had gotten rich freighting between Santa Fe and Chihuahua. He had lost mules worth about four thousand dollars, but that made little difference to him. He regarded the trip as a lark.

Robert knew he was not crazy. He had two hallucinations but they seemed real to him only when he was asleep. In one of them he saw a slim white body pegged to the ground and writhing. . . . In the other he chased an Indian and caught him and pulled his head off as one might pull the head off a chicken. The Indian's neck stretched to an astonishing length and then popped with a great

[116]

spurt of blood. He would wake up feeling the blood on his hands and then find it was sweat. This nightmare always waked him as soon as he fell asleep. . . . Loss of sleep and coffee made his head feel queer but he knew what he was doing all right. He was going out to shoot Indians. He didn't let himself build any hopes of seeing Elizabeth again and he tried not to think of how she might be if he did. . . . He felt all the time that he had killed her.

Soon after midnight they made a camp where no one was allowed to talk or smoke or light fire and a horse that started to whinney was gagged. Then they moved again a few miles, horses were left in a hollow under guard and all the rest went up a high hill in the dark making little noise.

The Utes were in front and then came the soldiers. Robert and his companions were told to stay behind the lines but Maguffey led them around behind a clump of brush so they could look down into the valley.

When it began to get light they could see first the shine of the wide shallow river and then the Indian tepees as white cones with smoke-blackened tops. About a hundred and fifty of them made a half circle on a wide grassy flat with dark low cottonwood timber between them and the river. It was the dead moment of early morning before birds began to sing.

It got lighter and they could see dogs moving

among the tepees. A thin smoke went up from inside one. A few horses were tethered in the camp and a herd of them a few hundred yards up the valley began to graze. An Indian boy appeared riding toward the herd to round it up and bring it in.

That was evidently what they were waiting for.

The Ute scouts suddenly went over the brow of the hill on horseback in a dead run, waving blankets, yelling enough for a hundred and shooting in the air. The soldiers on foot came running behind them and fell down flat on the crest to shoot.

The camp in the valley seemed to fly into frenzied fragments. Indians popped out of every tepee, all running in different directions, all yelling. Women screeched, children bawled, men shouted, dogs barked. Horses broke loose and ran and the herd stampeded through one end of the camp while the Utes swept through the other. The soldiers on the hill top began a fire that crackled along their line and showed as sharp red spurts and blue smoke hanging in still air.

The camp in the valley became a great blur of dust filled with moving figures, nearly all of them women, children, dogs and horses. As always in an Indian camp the stock and the families outnumbered the warriors ten to one.

Robert, with a nervous finger on a trigger,

couldn't see anything to shoot at, couldn't get a bead. Gilchrist had one of the new Winchesters and he was lying flat on his belly shooting as fast as he could work the gun, not stopping to aim. Maguffey rolled over and addressed him.

"What the hell are you shooting at?" he demanded. "I can't see nothin' a feller could hope to hit from here."

Gilchrist emptied his gun, snapped it a couple of times and then subsided, looking foolish.

The Indians were not as crazy as they looked. Already most of the women and children were splashing across the shallow river, nearly out of range. Some of them were on foot and some on ponies. Many ponies carried two and some three. Bullets plopped in the water and a few Indians fell. Hidden warriors were shooting back from the cottonwood fringe to cover the retreat and another band of them were going over the hill on the other side with most of the ponies.

The soldiers ran down the hill and into the deserted camp. They charged the cottonwoods shooting and silenced the hidden Indians.

Blue-coated men and brown naked men were now running around among the tepees in a brief moment of pillage before the officers got control again.

"Come on," said Maguffey, who seemed to get no excitement out of anything. "Le's go down there and see what we killed. They nearly all got clean away . . ."

The first tepee they came to was a large one made of buffalo hides with queer designs painted all over the outside. A light Springfield wagon stood behind it and on the ground near the door were some little bows and arrows such as Indian boys play with. Maguffey pulled open the front flap and looked in and Robert looked over his shoulder.

Two of the Ute squaws had gotten there before them. One of them at the back of the lodge was bending over the body of a very old Indian man with white hair. When their eyes got used to the dim light they could see the squaw had cut the old man's throat and was taking some kind of necklace off him. Maguffey went over and looked.

"This old boy was stone blind," he remarked. "He never had no chance."

The squaw looked up at him with frightened furtive eyes, clutching her trophy. Maguffey took it and examined it, showed it to Robert with a snort of disgust. It was a medicine bag made of a human scrotum, nicely tanned and decorated. Maguffey threw it away and the squaw went and got it again.

Indians and soldiers were still rustling around the camp. Most of them were laughing and excited, holding up plunder and shouting to each other.

They were just like bad boys raiding the lunch baskets at a picnic. . . . A bugle blew and they all ran toward the other end of the camp.

"I don't see many dead ones," Maguffey commented. "Of course they carry off their dead if they can." He looked around. "There's one over there." He pointed to a huddle of clothing that lay half way between the camp and the river.

They went and looked. A squaw had been hit in the knee by a bullet that smashed the joint and ranged down so that the whole of her lower leg was a mass of blood. She lay on her back and rolled slightly from side to side, moaning softly in a regular rhythm. When she saw them she got up on an elbow and pointed and gestured toward a little bunch of willows about fifty feet away. Robert went and looked under it and found an Indian boy about two years old lying there in the shade. It wore a little buckskin smock, trimmed with beads, and tiny moccasins. When it saw him it shut its eyes tightly and began to squall. Robert picked it up.

Maguffey roared with laughter.

"Now you got a prisoner," he said. "Fine! What are you gonna do with him?"

Robert didn't know. He was embarrassed and bewildered. The young Comanchee went on yelling, and the effort made his nose bubble green all over his dirty face. He snuffled and gasped and yelled some more. Robert laid the baby down in

a patch of shade and carefully wiped its nose, which
made it yell all the more. It seemed to think he
was trying to smother it. Maguffey kept on laughing, but Robert was intent. He didn't know what
to do with the baby but he was glad to have something to bother him. It seemed to him that if the
baby would only stop yelling he wouldn't mind
having it in his arms. He put it down again in the
shadow of the tepee, snapped his fingers at it,
showed it his watch, whistled, tried all the methods
he had ever seen used to quiet babies. But this
baby scorned them all.

Robert became intensely absorbed in his effort
to capture the baby's attention. It seemed as though
only a small part of his mind was alive and that
little was all concentrated on the baby. He had a
piece of hard Mexican chocolate in his pocket. He
finally got this into the little brown fist and con-
veyed it to the expostulating mouth. He could see
the agonized knot of the small face relax as the
sweet touched the palate. The baby opened his
eyes, shut his mouth on the chocolate and regarded
Robert for the first time. It had a peculiarly grave
steady look. For a full minute they exchanged a
profound stare.

Maguffey had called a couple of soldiers with a
stretcher. They were carrying the squaw away.
Robert followed with the baby all the way back to
where the horses were corralled. The company

surgeon was there getting ready to cut a hand off a soldier who had been hit in the wrist. Three soldiers were dead and six wounded. The three dead lay in a row covered with a wagon sheet and the wounded were in the shade of a cottonwood waiting for help. A man, shot in the groin was groaning and rolling but the others were quiet. One man with his shirt almost soaked in blood, smoked a cigar calmly.

"I reckon I've got mine," he said. "But I'll be damned if I can feel anything."

The doctor, hot and harassed, swore when he saw the squaw.

"Put her down there in the shade and give her a drink of water," he said. "I'll fix her up when I get around to it . . ."

"What shall I do with the baby?" Robert asked.

The doctor was petulant. "For Christ's sake, don't ask me!"

Robert finally left the baby lying in the shade, slobbering over its chocolate. It seemed happy and unconcerned now.

When they got back to the top of the hill the Indian camp was a great bonfire. A few soldiers tended it while the rest formed in marching order with a skirmish line ahead.

They could see the lay of the battle as on a map. The other Indian camp was just visible about two miles down the valley and the Indians were gath-

ering between. They were not going to run. Warriors of the two camps were organizing to make
a fight and there were several hundred of them.

Robert began to realize he was about done. His
knee joints twitched when he walked and black
shapes danced like a horde of imps before his eyes.
Maguffey was also through fighting Indians. His
two hundred pounds and his high heeled riding
boots had done for his feet. The two seekers for
revenge sat down in the shade of a rock to watch
and wait.

At the foot of the hill soldiers were deploying,
running forward and falling flat to fire. Behind the
lines howitzers unlimbered. . . . Far down the
valley mounted Indians gathered in a cloud of
dust. Now and then a solitary horseman rode out
in front, and shook the lifted shield of defiance.
Shrill battle yells rose above the deep rolling chorus
of a war chant.

On came Indians at a slow trot. Then suddenly
half of them circled and charged across the line of
fire, swung low behind their horses' necks and shot
back at shooting soldiers. Ponies fell and rolled
and dismounted Indians ran for their own lines,
but their charge held the advance of the troops,
and they charged again and again, in larger numbers, sweeping closer. They were as hard to hit
as swallows on the wing and three horses were
killed for every Indian.

Howitzers coughed and a shell exploded half-way to the Indian lines, throwing up a great spurt of earth. They coughed again and a shell broke in the midst of the milling horsemen, shattering a charge. . . . It was only the howitzers that held them.

For a while the battle hung balance, the soldiers holding their skirmish line but advancing it not at all. Then wind blew from the south, straight from red to white, as though savage chants had been answered by savage Gods. Running Indians waving torches set the grass afire and the soldiers faced a new enemy of boiling blue smoke edged with pale fire, running toward them across the whole width of the valley. Behind the smoke screen Indians charged again, charged so close that some fell dead within fifty feet of the skirmish line. They swept forward with the wind when it freshened and back when it fell. They were like sprites of the prairie fire that showed and vanished in forms of blowing smoke. Soldiers ran back, blinded. Howitzers could not find their mark.

Bugles blew again, bugles of defeat. With pickets out and firing and the howitzers protecting their rear, the troops fell back toward the hills and their horses.

Robert, stumbling over burnt grass with smoke in his eyes, heard the bugles sound retreat, heard the Indian yell of triumph, knew the savage line

[125]

would never be broken, knew the Indian camp would keep its secret now. . . .

It was nearly dark when the troops reached their horses and the weary ride homeward began.

Picket rifles still cracked in the dusk. Faraway shrill yells came to their ears. Against the wide red sash of the sunset, along the ridge across the valley, they saw silhouettes of Indian horsemen riding the other way. The could see blankets and shields waved in signal and hear deep chants of victory that rose and fell in a vast diffuse chorus, seeming only half human, as though the prairie sang with her children in the voices of winds and rivers.

Robert rolled and wobbled in his saddle, holding the pommel to keep from falling. Faraway savage voices were a lullaby and his life was a hope of sleep.

THIRD PART
RAILROAD

Chapter One

THOSE were the days when rails first crossed the Rockies—when a young and lusty nation, coming back from war, found the virgin West lying ready. . . . Days when red-headed Greeley shouted "Go West, young man," when Patti sang and Edwin Forrest spouted and Walt Whitman wrote, when crowds gaped at Tom Thumb and the dog-faced boy, when Evangeline brought a tear to the eye and Bill Nye shook the roof. . . . Rails across a continent had been an improbable dream, a hope too high. Now they were a miraculous fact, the proof that dreams come true.

Rails seemed the way to everything men wanted —to land and gold and freedom—but they were more than that. At every railhead orators mounted flat cars and told the people what the railroad meant—progress, expansion, empire, manifest destiny, sea to sea, liberty enlightening the world, the stars and stripes forever . . . hooray!

In those days men believed in liberty as they believed in God. Progress was salvation and work was a holy cause. . . . The rails went west on a wave of faith and energy nothing could check.

First went surveyors. Little parties strung out

long, following a compass line across a wilderness, waving red flags, driving stakes, building stone monuments to mark the way for the rails.

Red Cloud, great Sioux Chief, rode to meet them, sitting his horse proudly with feathered painted warriors behind him. He raised his hand.

"You must go back," he said. "You are scaring the buffalo."

Nine surveyors beat off three hundred Sioux. Many a man dropped on the compass line. One boy the Indians thought was dead got up when they lifted his hair, killed an Indian and brought his own scalp home in a bucket of water. . . .

After surveyors came the grading gangs. Those were tough babies!—shanty Irish come starving from the old exhausted sod. General Sherman said the whisky they drank would kill all the Indians within three hundred miles. It didn't but the graders almost did. A hungry Irishman is tough meat even for a Sioux. When they had no Indians to fight they fought each other to keep in trim. Supply trains bristled rifles and rifles were stacked by the men while they worked. Indians got away with the mules but not with the Irish. . . .

Indians sat back on the hills and saw the first trains run. Indians went down and stretched a strong rawhide rope from pony to pony across the tracks to stop the iron horse. Indians got heap big surprise.

Indians charged the iron horse waving blankets
to scare it, yelling their war yells and the iron
horse plowed right through them, never shying,
spouting rifle fire.

Then Indians got wise. Turkey Leg's Cheyennes
bent up the rails, piled ties and rocks in the road,
sat down and waited. A mixed freight hit the trap,
threw the fireman into his own woodburning fire
box, piled up in the ditch. Indians came yelling
down, killed the crew, raided the box cars, found
wet goods and dry goods, got Indian crazy drunk,
dressed up in ladies bonnets and shawls, tied bolts
of cloth to ponies' tails and ran races with a hundred yards of calico streaming in the wind. They
set the train on fire and danced a scalp dance round
a flame that lit the sky. So Indians danced at their
own funeral.

With the rails and the pay-car came the roaring towns that fed the end of the track—Cresco,
Truckee, Lovelocks, Winnemucca, Wells, Taono,
Green River, Julesberg, Wasatch. Hell on wheels
they called them. Men in those towns were drunk on
hope and money before they took a drink. They
were out to spend and ready to shoot and the law
was what you made it. They were men of many
kinds—tracklayers and tie-cutters, gold-hunters
and land-hunters, bull-whackers and mule-skinners
of the doomed wagon trade, soldiers, remittance

[131]

men, British younger sons, real estate sharks, blacklegs, liquor dealers, tin horns. There were no ladies and few women but many "girls." . . . Those were the booming golden days of prostitution when whores were almost the only women in towns of ten thousand men, when fortunes were spent on them, men were killed for them, when they were wooed by everything from waterboys to millionaires. Painted black and carmine, loaded with gold and diamonds, they dragged voluminous silks and satins through the mud and dust of swarming narrow streets. Pearl-handled Derringers dangled from black ribbons round their necks and they flashed stilettoes and bank rolls out of silk stockings. . . . Those were the days when a fancy woman was fancy and a good woman took in wash. . . .

And those were the days when gamblers got at last most of everybody's cash. They were the dressiest citizens in town and the deadliest and they barked their challenge in every bar.

"Come on, you rondocoolo sports!"

"Keeno to-night!"

Also monte, poker, chuck-a-luck and faro, with players fighting to get to the tables where reticent gentlemen in frock coats presided with six shooters and gathered money with rakes.

After the first few towns had risen and died, they began shipping them out from Chicago in knockdown style. You could order a brownstone front by mail and two boys could build a town with a screw driver. Saloons started building Friday morning and opened for business Saturday night, with kerosene burning by the barrel in bright tin lamps and liquor running so fast you could smell it all over town. Silver fell in a steady shower on bars and tables. Fifty professors hammered fifty pianos and bareback beauties pranced in fifty dance halls. Six shooters popped. They shot a man for hogging the gravy and killed a cook for burning the pie. Vigilantes rode and broken necks dangled from trees and bridges. . . .

The pay-car moved on and everything followed it, portable houses and all, on trains and in wagons and on foot, leaving a station house, a water tank, a mountain of rusty oyster cans and a graveyard.

The railroads had to sell the land along the tracks and they began to comb the world for settlers. The Santa Fe sent to Europe and got fifteen thousand Mennonites to come to Kansas. From neat shaded little homes they came to scare the antelope off bare sunburned prairie. One drove his wagon ten miles from the rails and stopped where not a tree grew and nothing moved but a buzzard

[133]

in the sky. "Why do you stop here?" his wife asked, and he said, "This is where we live." The woman cried for a while and then she climbed out of the wagon and began to cook supper.

Drought burned the corn of the Mennonites and grasshoppers came in a rolling cloud along the ground and left it bare. But the Mennonites stuck and others followed. Men began selling cornfields in Missouri and Iowa for a hundred an acre and buying the prairie in Kansas and Colorado for five. . . . In those days men wanted all the land they could get and they craved to break wild land and make it yield.

So the Santa Fe crept across the prairie. Then Leadville boomed and trains began running packed both ways taking in the flush and bringing out the broke. Everybody was heading for Colorado, in those days, from Irish labor to Lord Dunraven, who went with a retinue to slaughter grizzlies and wanted a piece of the Rockies for a park.

The Santa Fe and the Denver and Rio Grande fought for the Royal Gorge to the West and Raton Pass to the South. They shipped in bad men from Dodge with rifles, and rival graders slugged it out on the right of way.

The Santa Fe won Raton Pass. Slow and late it crawled down the Rio Grande.

It followed the trail the Indians had made, the trail conquistadores in iron armor had followed, and after them the mountain men—the trail the wagons and coaches had widened into a road.

Rails crept down the Rio Grande, prodded sleepy 'dobe towns into sudden frantic life. The stage from Los Vegas to Albuquerque made its last trip. Uncle Dick Wooton closed his toll road. The great Murphy wagons dropped their tongues on the ground forever. . . . Once more the good old days were gone.

Chapter Two

THE day the first train pulled out for the East was a day of celebration. The program would begin at noon with speeches from a flat car draped in bunting and it would end when the last drunk got home the next morning.

Robert drove to New Town behind his new team of bays hitched to his new carriage and he wore a new suit and a new hard hat. A gold watch chain a foot long, looped across both sides of his vest, anchored a hundred-dollar solid gold watch in his pocket.

Lacking a family he had for guests his old German housekeeper, Mrs. Latz, and her daughter Annie who had just come back from school in St. Louis. He had his doubts about the propriety of taking them with him, but it would be too bad for the women to miss the whole show.

Mrs. Latz wore a black silk dress, big as a thunder cloud in the skirt and stiff enough to stand alone. She carried a little black silk parasol and wore long black gloves with the fingers cut off at the knuckle. She climbed into the back seat, spread her skirt, lifted her head, folded her hands and assumed a rigid expression of defiant elegance.

Robert struggled with a smile as he got into the front seat. To him she was a good deal less impressive in her black silk than she was in calico in the kitchen with her hands on her hips, scolding him in a splutter of German-English for being late again to supper. The old woman ruled him in his own house. He had no say there. But he had come to depend upon her so completely that he could never bring himself to let her go.

"Annie!" she addressed her daughter always with asperity. "You sit in front and don't giggle!"

Annie giggled and climbed in beside Robert. He told himself he didn't want her there, but he could see the old woman needed the whole of the back seat for her skirt so he didn't dare to object.

Annie wore a modest blue dress that left her arms bare to the elbow and showed a little of her neck. She sat primly, too, looking straight ahead, but with an expression of eager childish delight. Robert kept glancing at her sidelong as he drove. He could not get used to the change in her. She had gone away to school a pale skinny little girl with big eyes, addicted to handsprings and all-day suckers, and she had come back a young woman of striking curve and color. She had not grown much taller but she had grown in every other direction. She had budded like a twig in the spring. As she jostled gently beside him on the seat she seemed alive with a life that might break through the tight poplin of her bodice. . . . Although she stood little taller she sat higher than before. She had more to sit on.

The same sudden change happened to every girl but he had never noticed it before. He couldn't help noticing it this time. . . . When he had first employed Mrs. Latz, five years before, he and Annie became good friends. She hung around the store and he gave her candy. He had thought of her as a daughter he might have had if things had been different. . . . When he smoked his pipe in the evenings on the porch she used to come and sit on his lap sometimes. . . . Annie on his lap now. . . . Well. . . . He had paid for her education, insisted on doing it, because she was so unmistakably bright and there were no schools in the town worth going to and it seemed a shame to let the priests get hold of her. Now she was a properly educated young woman, could play the piano, speak a little French and had perfect manners that would have been stiff except for the white beam of her smile and the dance of light in her eyes. She had a rather flat nose but her eyes and her smile would have triumphed over any nose. Her hands were slim and beautiful and that in spite of all the hard work she had done with them helping her mother in the kitchen, and she had such slim feet none of the shoes in the store would fit her. Where did she get such slim pretty hands and feet? Not from her mother certainly. Mrs. Latz had hands like a man. And not from old man Latz, who had driven mules for him in seventy-one and died on the road. . . . Thick-jointed heavy-footed peasants both of them. . . . He tried to imagine Mrs. Latz having an affair with some high-bred lover long ago but he could not even imagine her young and the mere thought of any scandal in connection with Mrs. Latz seemed an outrage, so he gave up the problem of where Annie got her hands and feet. . . . Her figure too for that matter. . . . Well he had educated her and here she was. . . . Nothing more he could do for her except try to get her well married, and the sooner the better. If he kept her around the house people would talk and he was a prominent citizen now. Besides he was thinking of getting married himself and that would mean the departure of both Mrs. Latz and Annie.

Telling the old woman to go would be a hard day's work. . . . But meantime what to do with Annie? He couldn't give a party and introduce his cook's daughter to his friends. In the old days, something of the kind might have been possible but not since the railroad officials had come to town and the Robinsons had built their house. . . . Now they had Society. . . . The grand ball in the hall over the wool house that night was going to be the first great society event in the history of New Town. Rush orders for dress suits had been

put through and they had wired Denver for a special shipment of white ties and gloves. . . .

Annie hadn't been home a week before Mrs.
Latz invited Otto Schwentker over, fed him in
the kitchen and he stayed all evening talking to
Annie. Annie seemed to like him well enough. Robert had heard them laughing till late. But it irritated him. Had he educated the girl to have her
marry a piece of beef? Otto was a young immi-
grant carpenter, a thick red young man with a
heavy accent and stubby fingers. Robert had told
the old lady frankly he didn't like it, Schwentker
wasn't good enough for Annie. She asked him who
was good enough, said Otto was a nice steady young
man who drank nothing but beer. Her old-fashioned German idea was to marry Annie off right
away quick. Disgusting. Just like leading a mare
to the stud. Why couldn't she let the girl alone for
a while? . . . Well, no. . . . Something had to
be done about Annie. She made an unmistakable
impression of urgent destiny. And the old lady was
introducing her daughter to the only people she
knew. Did he, after all, have the right to object?
It was a problem. Anything was a problem when
his conscience got to working on it. . . . He had
blundered so much, hurt so many. . . . Elizabeth
. . . don't think. . . .

Chuckholes slowed the carriage and shook him
back to the business of driving. A mile of rutty

road, ruined by heavy hauling, separated the old town from the new one and the railroad station. They had tried hard to have the road touch the town but they were only laughed at. Railroads turned aside for no man. Everything was moving to New Town now. They would have to move the store. . . .

New Town was just two streets that crossed. They were lined with tent houses, yellow unpainted shacks, stores and saloons of glaring tin and raw lumber with false fronts twenty feet high. Seven saloons were doing good business. They all had faro, poker, Keeno and Monte and five of them had dance halls behind and painted women with short hair.

The whores and the gamblers had begun to come in with the tie-cutters two years before and had multiplied ever since on railroad money like flies around a growing leak in a sorghum barrel. Gambling and the liquor business were the town's leading industries now. Tom's saloon, the Silver Dollar, was the biggest and best and had the reputation of being the only one where the games were straight. Tom was clearing a hundred dollars a day. Robert had refused to join him in that venture. They still owned the store together but it was a minor interest to both of them. Tom was trying to corner the liquor business and Robert killed horses traveling between his sawmill in the mountains and the boom town of Socorro where he had a quarter interest in a silver mine. They hadn't begun to mill ore yet but they had sunk a shaft and knew it was there . . . silver free in the rock. . . . God only knew how much . . . millions maybe!

His blood pounded like a stamp mill when he thought of it. Not that he wanted millions, either, but just to find it that way! It had cost him nineteen dollars. That was his share of the grub stake four of them gave little Eli Hughes, thinking it charity. He would never forget the day Little Eli came back and unpacked a dusty burro and poured out a big bag of rock shot through and through with shining metal. "Well, boys, there it is and there's tons more where that come from." Little Eli, who had punched a burro across the hills for fifteen years without finding a thing! People kept him going for a joke. And now he swaggered around drunk wearing a bright blue suit and a twenty-dollar hat. He had a girl and packed a gun and had shot a man in what passed for a fair fight. Silver had ruined Eli. His only hope was to go broke and back to the hills. . . . But silver was a gamble and lumber was a sure thing and if Robinson gave him the railroad contract. . . . Talk to him to-night but not about lumber. Talk to her too. No need. She never stopped talking herself. Listen then. . . . A million feet of yellow pine!

. . . He could reach that much without moving his mill. . . .

Silver and lumber filled his mind. They filled his body with a never-ending tingle of excitement. He lived in the screech of a ripsaw, the smell of pitch, the feverish talk of the silver town. He gutted mountains and stripped them. He raped the earth. He lived in a rush of power visibly conquering rock and tree, making wheels turn and men sweat. And his power grew on its own conquest. More money, more things to do. . . . He was going to marry Emily Robinson if ever she stopped talking long enough to let him ask. . . . And not to get a contract, either, and not because he loved her but because she belonged to the new life that had come with the rails. He was going to marry railroads and lumber for they were his life and he was in no mood for love. . . . Love was far back there, a faint and seldom memory of pain and thrill, a thing that left a man weak and loosened. He was done forever with staring at the moon. He was nearly forty.

Wooden sidewalks four feet above the ground lined Railroad Avenue. Under them dogs and drunks slept and bewildered Indians squatted. A crowd of restless heels drummed on them to-day. Railroad labor was everywhere—blue shirted red-necked men, slow of foot and muscle bound. Lithe brown men in wide hats jingled their spurs along

the boards, and whole Mexican families trooped
by in single file, the men in gaudy new store clothes,
the blackshawled women with bundles of proven-
der on their heads, leading children by the hand.
Half the crowd were men of the new time—law-
yers, gamblers, railroad men, saloon keepers, real
estate agents—in white collars, frock coats and hard
hats. Gamblers all flashed diamonds and you could
see yards and yards of heavy gold watch chains
looped across prosperous stomachs with pendant
golden figures of horses, women and wild beasts
with ruby and emerald eyes.

Buggies and carriages kept the fine summer dust
in circulation. Among the scrawny familiar teams
of the Mexicans and the jogging cow ponies were
many fine highheaded trotters and pacers shipped
in from the East—satiny bays, chestnuts and sor-
rels hitched to buggies and light carriages. Many
of them were driven by women dressed in bright
silks that caught the sun, with painted faces,
bleached hair blowing in the wind and diamonds
showing on their arms and hands. They drove up
and down behind snorting foam-flecked thorough-
breds, speaking to no one but looked at by all,
wearing expressions of haughty contempt. A man
from another world would have thought they
owned the town.

The town had gone wild but not as wild as other
railroad towns. Here the rails had hit a civiliza-

tion, not a desert. Trouble started when the tie-cutters began to pour in and get drunk every Saturday night. Three new dance halls opened to take their money and men were knifed and shot. One drunk rode his horse into the store of Jayson and Foote and demanded cigars. While Robert gave him a handful, Diego Aragon pulled him off his horse from behind, took his gun away and kicked him eleven feet as ascertained by subsequent measurement, remarking as he did so that no goddam gringo was going to shoot up this Mexican town. Then they elected Diego Sheriff. He was running pretty wild in the new dance halls and there was opposition, but Tom and Robert backed him and the people who owed them money were enough then to carry any election. That was the making of Diego and the taming of the tough. With Diego it was a personal matter. He was out to show that no railroad or anything else could come in and shake up a town that had been founded by the Aragons and ruled by them for a hundred years. Ten tin-horns shut themselves up in a room at Sunnyside, got liquored to the gills and sent word for Diego to come and get them. And Diego came and kicked the door down and nobody dared to flash a gun because nobody wanted to die. . . . Diego was broad-minded and willing for everybody to have a good time in his own way but he drew the line at gunplay and frowned on crooked games. To work all their dirty tricks the gamblers had to boss a town and they didn't boss this one. They were going to run a man of their own for Sheriff against Diego. . . . It was war between the gamblers and the old-timers. . . . Also between the whores and the wives, who were just beginning to make themselves felt. The allied wives were giving the grand ball that night. Everybody who could get in would go to the ball first and down the line afterwards.

Jim Hepburn and Bert Lagrange were driving their English dogcart up and down the street, with two fat bay cobs hitched tandem, their heads martingaled high and their tails bobbed to the size of a whisk broom. The boys both wore checker-board suits and hard hats and Hepburn now and again lifted a whisky bottle with a blue ribbon around its neck and drank the health of any friend he could see in the crowd. Hepburn was a genuine British remittance man who dropped two hundred dollars a week on the town without doing a tap of work. Lagrange had a soft job procured by a rich papa running the street car line. . . . It was one car and two mules to haul Mexican labor to the railroad shops. . . . Jim and Bert were openly following Grace Tolliver who was driving around behind Two-forty, her trotting sorrell mare.

Since the railroad came many he knew had undergone astonishing transformations, but none had surprised him more than Grace. He remembered her first as a spoiled, restless child hanging around her father's hotel and then as a pretty sullen pouting girl of seventeen that Tom was courting. Tom was dog-poor then and Grace turned him down for a gambler named Wilky—one of the first that came to town. The next thing he knew the air was full of scandal, with old man Tolliver talking gun play. Grace and Wilky both disappeared, apparently in opposite directions. Robert knew that Grace had gone to San Francisco because Tom followed her there and came back sick and silent. It was whispered Grace had taken with her ten thousand dollars that old man Tolliver had scared out of Wilky, and it was also whispered that she had thrown her hat over the windmill. . . . They all knew it was true when she came brazenly back about a year later and opened the first high class sporting house the town had ever known. Before that there had been nothing but the cribs in Old Town where half-naked women crouched like waiting panthers in adobe doorways along a dimlit street, calling and beckoning, pouncing on helpless drunks. . . . The night Grace opened her place was a night of celebration. It was just as big a thing in the life of the town as opening a new bank or a new saloon. She was a local girl for one thing, but aside from that, everybody felt she had promoted an important local improvement. With

[147]

ten men coming to town for every woman, prostitution was the real social life and Grace lent it elegance. Her parlor was furnished in red plush with mirrors all around the wall and a hand-painted picture over the mantel of a naked lady reclining pensive on an emerald sward and billowing toward heaven with a mountainous hip. Her girls, all imported from San Francisco and picked for their looks, appeared in low-neck evening gowns and comported themselves like ladies. A "professor" in a dress suit hammered the piano and a negro maid with a little lace dingus on her head served drinks at a dollar a shot. No rough conduct was tolerated there. Prospectors and cowboys from the hills were awed and hushed in Grace's parlor as though it had been a church and could hardly believe that three dollars would purchase the favors of such haughty exquisites as met them here. . . . Grace was not only a friend of refinement and good order but she was also a shrewd business woman who owned real estate, had an account in the new First National Bank and loaned money where it would do the most good. She even had a little political influence. Moreover, her figure was already famous from El Paso to Denver. Its voluptuous pink abundance was the sensuous ideal of men who liked their beef steaks thick and their liquor straight. She was no longer a market commodity but a Madame who chose her favorites. If she changed these often it was only because they wore out, financially and physically. She was not to be had for cash alone. Bets were laid as to how long Jim Hepburn would last with the Bank of England to back him. . . .

The crowd was gathering around the tracks now. There would be a speech by Robinson, the train would pull out, and then there would be some more speeches by local orators. The platform around the little red station house was packed solid with people who jostled, stood on tiptoe and stretched their necks like turkeys. Mexicans in a long row had pre-empted the top of a board fence and boys were up telegraph poles and a cotton-wood tree. Carriages, buggies, buckboards and wagons were lined up on both sides of the track and many horsemen sat at ease, leaning back on one stirrup with a negligent leg across the saddle. . . . Stars and stripes were all over the flat car and Robinson stood up beside a little table with a white china pitcher and a glass on it. In his long frock coat and his white mutton chop whiskers he was a perfect emblem of respectability and money conquering the wild.

Few could hear what he said but all knew his sentiments. Isolated words flew out to the most distant ears, welcome as scraps to hungry dogs. . . . Progress . . . expansion . . . empire . . . civilization . . . millions . . . gold!

Everytime he stopped to mop sweat and swallow water applause filled the moment. Ladies clapped and men shouted. He had but to lift his arms to lift their voices. He was the leader in a communal chant of hope and triumph.

When he had climbed off the flat car and before the last cheers had died, the engine whistle gave its loud wild scream, its bell began to clang and from its tall topheavy smoke stack came a great black cloud and a heavy cough. About half of the Mexicans on the fence, many of whom had come from afar to see their first train, were observed to lean suddenly backward and disappear. Horses jumped, backed and snorted. Men leapt to bridle reins, their mouths open in a shout that was completely drowned in the noise of the engine.

Robert's bays tossed their heads and proceeded to back straight away from the black terror. They would either upset the carriage or back it into another team. He gave them a sharp cut with the whip, they reversed like rabbits and sprang into a run, smashing the carriage across the tracks, scattering the crowd, barely missing a wagon, and thundering up the long white road that led to the mountains. As he lay back on the reins Robert heard a wild scream from Mrs. Latz and felt Annie's arms tighten around his neck and her cheek press against his left ear. He tried to shake her off but she stuck like a sandbur while he rocked in his seat, sawing the mouths of the frightened horses, trying to break their stride.

The steep hill and the deep sand worked with him. About a quarter of a mile from the tracks he brought the team to a stop, breathing terror through wide fluttering nostrils.

He had not been scared but he was irritated. He had heard some loud laughter as they crossed the tracks and his mind held a picture of himself bouncing high in the air, with his hat down over his nose, Mrs. Latz yelling like an Indian and Annie hanging around his neck. Everybody had seen them, including the Robinsons. . . . He had had his doubts about bringing the women along, anyway. . . . He turned to Annie with something sharp on his tongue but her expression shut his mouth. She was flushed crimson, her eyes wide and shining, her lips parted.

"Wonderful!" she barely breathed. "You're so strong!"

Robert snorted . . . but he began to think he had done pretty well to stop a runaway team of blooded horses with one woman half strangling him and another screeching in his ear. . . . Mrs. Latz was lying back in her seat muttering German as she always did when moved by strong feeling.

He drove back slowly, made a wide circle around the crowd and pulled up inconspicuously behind it. Another flat car had been brought up by a switch engine and one prominent citizen after another climbed aboard it, waved his arms and shouted mighty words to the hot unflagging applauders. From his new position Robert could not catch a single sentence complete. He was bored but he felt bound to see the program through. Mrs. Latz, exhausted by terror, was dozing in the back seat. He was reluctant to disturb her and afraid every minute that she would disgrace him with one of her long rippling snores.

Annie had pulled out a tiny mirror. Hiding it in the cup of her hand she fussed intently with her heavy brown hair, disarranged by her wild ride. With deft slim fingers she captured errant strands and tucked them into place. Robert watched her lazily, finding her much more amusing than the speeches. When she had done with her hair she began to look around and he could see that she was covertly studying every woman within range of her eye. Now and again she glanced back at the little glass. Robert could almost feel her measuring her young strength against others. She was so intent that she never noticed him. In the mirror he caught a glimpse of her full face with its grave expression of absorbed self-consciousness. He had a strange momentary illusion of entering into Annie's mind. He felt the thrill, half reminiscent, half vicarious, of youth marching to its first great encounter. . . . Two young fellows he didn't know, sitting in a buggy twenty feet away, began to stare at her. A horseman was watching her, too, from under the brim of a wide hat. In fact, Annie's budding front and rosy cheeks were becoming a cynosure for a small circle of bored auditors. Aware of their eyes, she stiffened, looking straight ahead, and he could see the corners of her mouth wrestling with a smile.

The speeches had dragged on for more than an hour and now, God help them all, Old Judge Turnbull was laboriously lifting his two hundred pounds of senile loquacity onto the platform. Now, unless someone simply pulled him down by the coat tails, they would be in for a practically endless dissertation on the Democratic party and the principles of Thomas Jefferson. For five years the Judge had devoted all his time to organizing the Democratic party and it didn't exist—less now than ever, because the railroad was Republican.

Now he stepped forward and raised aloft the hand of the practiced orator, bidding for the attention of the multitude. From a thousand throats there went up an enormous cheer, accompanied by a thunder of boot heels on wagon bottoms, the cracking of whips and loud whistling through the teeth. Speech was impossible for several minutes. When the rumpus died down the Judge again advanced a step and again raised his imperative right hand, and once more a wild concerted yell forestalled his utterance. A third time he made his preliminary gesture with unfailing grace and this time the switch engine blew a loud blast, a puff of smoke leapt from its stack, and the Judge, his hand still lifted, his mouth visibly open, was transported rapidly two hundred yards down the track. . . . The program was over.

Chapter Three

Iᴛ took both the women to get him ready for the ball. Annie put the studs and cuff links in his dress shirt while Mrs. Latz set a wash boiler and two kettles full of water on the kitchen range so he could have a hot bath.

He had never worn a dress suit before and he felt both uncomfortable and foolish as he put it on. The irrepressible bulge of the shirt and the grip of the collar under his ears were especially annoying to him and he felt as though he could never get through the evening without spotting his front. It seemed to him he had no business in this thing. But when he glanced at himself in the mirror he was pleasantly surprised to find how much better he looked than he felt. In fact he was more impressed with his own good looks than he ever had been before. And he was glad he looked so much less than his years. He had shaved off his beard just a few months ago. He was lean as ever and had all his hair when so many men his own age were getting pot-bellied or bald or both. Just in the last few years he had begun to feel pleased when he heard himself mentioned as a young man. . . .

Both of the women followed him to the door, Mrs. Latz beaming and proud, picking a bit of lint off his coat, pulling his vest down, making him feel like a kid being started for Sunday school by his Ma.

It was hot in the long hall over the wool house which was used by the town for all large gatherings. The place was too crowded and forty lamps with tin reflectors were equal to a stove. The smell of wool and green hides came up through the floor and fought with the sweetness of perfumed ladies. But this occasion was a sprout of social energy that nothing could wilt. Everyone wore a look of beaming resolution and as the crowd gathered, appropriate conversation went forward like the march of a conquering army.

Skirts were full that year and dragged the ground and busts were bound in whalebone. Only arms and shoulders showed like those of brave swimmers above a swirling surf of multicolored silk and satin. Hair was piled high and often one woman wore the hair of three. Men in their dress suits seemed small and accessory beside the lift and spread of their mates, but they outnumbered the women two to one. Ladies still were scarce.

All were busy now filling out large cardboard programs with small tasselled pencils. Perspiring menials passed through the hall bearing freezers of ice cream, snow covered peaks of angel cake, stacks of sandwiches and platters of chicken salad. A committee of ladies had labored for days on the refreshments and they were such as had never been seen in the town before. Ice cream and cake here made their first assault against the deeply intrenched forces of free lunch and hard liquor. The hands of the pure to-night came bearing angel food for men.

Robert and Tom shook hands and stood side by side looking it all over. Both of them were stags. Tom eased a high and cutting collar off a sweating neck with his forefinger and pulled down a vest that showed a tendency to scale the bulge of his middle.

"Ain't this fine!" he said heartily. "This here is civilization! . . . It's due to be over at midnight sharp. Be sure and stay for the Kelly Club after the ladies go. We're gonna have some good stunts."

Professor DeMorro and his four piece orchestra rendered the overture to Faust which was received with a patter of refined applause. Then came the grand march, and spectators saw the greatest parade of beauty and fashion, of elegance and respectability the town had even known. Here was all of the old Spanish aristocracy—Aragons, Ortizes, Chaveses, Romeros and many more, with their ponderous wives and slim daughters—and here in addition were general managers, passenger agents, attorneys, bankers, a United States senator, a "big money man" from New York, a wool buyer from Boston and the females of all these species.

When the march broke up into waltzing couples the stags and miscellaneous onlookers broke into heavy applause. As it died down the wild rich shout of a locomotive whistle split the hush. A bell clanged and the heavy snort of the starting engine seemed to shake the floor. "Thar she goes!" shouted some unknown. They all laughed and then they started clapping again. . . . The railroad was part of the party.

The Lancers went off well but in the Virginia Reel a good many got lost and the thing turned into a comedy. The Schottische and the Polka they danced, too, but the waltz was what made the ball a success. Everybody could waltz.

About half way through the evening some couples began going out on the narrow balcony at the back of the hall. Robert made up his mind that when his dance with Emily Robinson came around he would try to lead her out there. . . . It was about time for a show-down.

He was nervous and tempted to go out and get

a drink but checked himself in time. The Robinsons were religious and the old man, he believed, was a teetotaller. The temperance movement in the East had come West with the railroad. At least there had been a temperance lecture in that very hall and he had heard of boys taking a pledge and something about lips that touch liquor shall never touch mine. Emily was probably not so strict as all that but she was a moral and religious young lady as she ought to be. The town needed morality and religion. Capital wouldn't come to a wild town. Too many wild track-end towns had flared up like grass fire and died down as quick. This place wasn't going to be another Dodge City or Abilene. It was going to be the greatest railroad center west of the Mississippi. They already had the shops. . . . Nothing gave a town such a look of permanence and dignity as a few brick churches. He had subscribed already to church funds of four different denominations. . . . Churches they needed and women—respectable married women, good homes, baby buggies—something to show the visitor besides saloons and red lights. . . .

While his mind thus strayed his eye followed the tall figure of Emily Robinson going through the Lancers with grace and precision, holding the train of her gown looped over her elbow so that it just cleared the floor and barely revealed the movement of her feet. . . . She had come with

[159]

her father. . . . Three times now he had been to
dinner at their new house, pride of the town, a big
blue frame sticking up out of the sunflowers with
a square lawn around it, kept alive by a Mexican
with a sprinkling can. Everybody saw the Robinson place as a forecast of the city that would be—
long rows of fine houses with lawns, cast iron deer,
stone hitching posts. . . .

The old man liked him, he was sure. Each time
he went there they talked till he left about railroads, coal mines and lumber, and he told about
the early days, his trading trip to the Apache country and how he nearly lost his life in a snow storm.
He was surprised to find himself regarded as a
man who had lived through almost incredible adventures.

When he talked Emily was visibly impressed.
Her rapt attention, her Ohs and Ahs, made him
feel large and unusual. . . . His relation with Emily
was a peculiar one. They had never exchanged an
intimate word, never called each other by their
first names, and yet he felt sure an understanding
existed between them, based on their mutual sense
of their fitness for each other. . . . The problem
was how to put that feeling into words. Something
about her tied him, hand and tongue. I love you he
could not say. My sincere regard and affection
would sound hollow. To put his arm around her—
to claim her as one might some women—was sim-

ply impossible. It would seem as sudden and un-
called-for as to hit her in the face.

Watching her he tried to guess her thought.
To him she presented a surface smooth and perfect as that of an egg. . . . What feeling hid behind that endless flow of talk, what body was
inside that concealing silk, that constricting whalebone? Some women seemed always about to break
out of their clothes but Emily belonged inside of
hers. The thought of Emily undressed was too ob-
scene for endurance . . . hard to imagine as a
bird without feathers. . . . How old? Hard to
guess but not less than thirty. That was all right.
He wanted a woman mature, dignified, able to en-
tertain important friends. He needed a wife as a
man afoot needs a horse and she was just what he
wanted. Everything she did filled him with admiration—the way she ran her father's house, enter-
tained, organized ladies into committees. She had
started the Library Fund and the Charitable As-
sociation. She had made the town ashamed of its
wooden sidewalks with nails sticking up that tore
dresses and drunken loafers lying underneath looking up through knot holes and lewd painted women
gallivanting down the streets behind fast horses
and three saloons to a block. . . . More than anyone else she deserved credit for this event, for the
dress suits and white ties, the ice cream and angel
food. She was refinement itself and that was what

they needed. Culture and capital . . . somebody
said it in a speech. . . . All the natural resources
in the world useless without. . . . And they went
together. . . . He was capital and Emily was
culture. . . .

Conscious of its dignity, capital bowed to culture. "I believe this is ours." Smiling a firm un-
breakable smile she rose to meet him. She rose
astonishingly high. Counting all the hair she wore
she was taller than he and her skirt was wide as a
door. He felt small as he circled her waist with a
large white silk handkerchief between his possibly
maculate hand and the silken perfection which en-
closed her back. With careful steps he trundled
her. . . . They danced, not with abandon, but
with dignity, adequately. She was whalebone under
his hand, perfume in his nose, a firm elbow limit-
ing an intimacy which he did not press, and a firm
pleasant voice talking without effort and without
pause. "Yes, it is warm, but isn't it lovely and such
a splendid crowd. I feel sure this is the beginning
of a real social life for the town. . . . Perfectly
delightful affairs. . . . We're planning a whole
series of grand balls for the library fund and a
musicale too . . . all the local talent. . . . There's
more than you might think . . ."

Nodding and yessing, he piloted cautiously,
watching over her shoulder to dodge possible col-
lision, moving his feet with care, conscious of her

toes. . . . He had been waltzing for seventeen years but not so slow. . . . He had learned in the little adobe hall in Old Town where he and Tom and Diego used to go nearly every Saturday night and with Maria's help he had mastered the fast choppy waltz of the Mexicans to Cucuracha played on an accordion. It was clinch and hop in those days. This slow gliding business was new to him. . . . Poetry of motion! . . . He felt like a man on a tight rope, every muscle tense. . . . There were some grand balls in those days, too, at the Aragons but nowhere near as grand as this. . . . It was at the common bailes where you paid a dollar that they had fun. The three of them used to ride out into the country, to Atrisco, Corrales, Pajarito, just to go to the bailes, stopping at every cantina on the way, riding home late whooping and yelling. . . . The time they had a fight in Corrales and Tom knocked the Alcalde cold. . . . Those were rough days and he was young. . . . Maria . . . Nina . . . Cucuracha. . . . Rasp of feet on a sanded floor, flicker of candles in smoky air, brown girls hugged in a tipsy whirl. . . .

The music stopped and he stood patting his white gloves together like the others, grinning and sweating, feeling he had done a hard thing well. . . . But now was the time. . . . As music started again he touched her arm.

[163]

"It's so warm. . . . Wouldn't you like to go out on the balcony a little while?"

Disconcerting words, a blow to be parried, a difficult question to settle quick. "Really I don't know . . . do you think? . . . Well ..." While she hesitated he looked her in the eye with a look full of resolution and meaning. For a moment the decision hung suspended as when two wrestlers rock and sway before the fall. Then her eyes dropped modestly before his bold commanding stare. "Well, all right . . ."

She wasn't perfectly sure. That was clear. She was compromising herself at his behest. He felt bigger and stronger as he steered her for the door, she glancing around nervously as they passed out into the dark. . . . Nobody there and a bench to sit on. . . . They sat.

He laid his arm along the back of the bench but she did not come within a foot of it. She sat stiffly erect, nervous fingers playing with a handkerchief in her lap. They sat in a heavy silence which she did nothing to break, for the first time, it seemed to him, since he had known her. . . . She was a wonderful conversationalist. Everybody that knew her agreed to that. When it came to throwing a bright remark into the middle of an awkward pause he had never seen her equal. He wished she would throw one now because he couldn't think of a thing. . . . He had a lot to say but he couldn't start. If

she had relaxed the least bit, if she had leaned back
against his arm, if her hand had strayed his way.
. . . But you couldn't make love to a woman that
looked as though she might jump over the railing
any minute. . . . He began to feel a little irritated. She wasn't thinking of him. She was thinking of the people inside and of what they were
thinking. . . . She wished she hadn't come. . . .
Well, could you blame her? A strong sense of
propriety was one of the things he admired. Probably he had done wrong to ask her to come. She was
the most prominent figure on the floor. . . . Everybody would notice. . . . He had dragged her out
here and now he sat dumb as a dead nigger in a
mudhole. The palms of his hands were sweating
and his throat was dry—sure signs he was losing
his nerve.

He had a queer feeling that he had been here
before . . . a vague memory of other times when
his hand and tongue had been suddenly paralyzed.
. . . Always the woman had broken through. . . .
If women had all been as proper as they were supposed to be. . . . And Emily was. . . . She put
it all up to him. . . .

From the constricted elegance of her waistline
to the feather in her hair she towered above the
billowing foothills of her skirt like a cool remote
mountain it would take a bold man to climb. He
was not a bold man.

[165]

He cleared his throat and with travail brought forth a feeble word.

"Emily . . ."

She turned sharply to look at him, leaning a little away, as though poised for flight.

"Yes . . ." There was a whisper of excitement at the end of the word. He had never called her Emily before.

"You don't mind my calling you Emily, do you?" He was warming to his work.

"Why no . . . not at all. I'm glad . . . Robert!" She gave a thin nervous laugh.

The music stopped and a group of people came laughing through the door, men manipulating silk handkerchiefs and women waving wide fans.

Emily rose suddenly, decisively.

"We must be going in," she said, and as they walked: "It's been awfully nice. I feel so much better for a little fresh air. Here comes dear father. You must come and see us . . . soon . . . Robert!"

She laughed again, arching her rather long neck and giving him a look almost rougish. Her laugh was high and rapid . . . like the whinny of a mare. . . . The comparison came into his mind and he brushed it out as being too vulgar.

"Thank you, I will. Just as soon as I can . . ."

Should have said Emily again but couldn't quite get it out. . . . It hadn't been such a fizzle after

all. He had made progress. . . . Next time. . . .
He took in a deep breath and blew it out with au-
dible emphasis. He felt immensely relieved that
that part of the evening was over. Home sweet
home the orchestra was playing. He looked forward to a good stiff drink and some cheese and
crackers and a cigar and the Kelly Club. . . . He
needed a little relaxation.

Chapter Four

WHEN the orchestra had packed up its instruments and all the good-nights had been said and hacks, carriages and buggies had rolled away with their skirted and slippered burdens, the long hall over the wool house began to fill again.

The night was not over, not by jugful. In the saloons along Railroad Avenue the taps and bottles were running a flood, poker games were getting tense and the keeno-callers droned their numbers to a growing crowd. Down in hookertown it was the shank of the evening with a dozen tin-panny pianos in full racket and a hundred voices calling hello dearie. . . . It was time for ladies to be abed but not for gentlemen.

A man needed no clawhammer coat to get into the Kelly Club. Most prominent citizens belonged but no good fellow was barred and this night almost every member brought a guest. Dress suits and flannel shirts met here and spurs rattled up the steps beside patent leathers. Gringo and Mexican, Jew and Italian made easy fraternity. Joe Carnetti, who had come to town with a hand organ and a monkey and now owned a big saloon, would never shine in the social life that was dawning. He had canceled his claim to gentility by marrying the whore that fed him when he was poor, but he was a leading member of the Kelly Club. So was Tony Schultz who had been a blacksmith before the railroad came and now turned over hardware, saddlery and harness to the tune of twenty thousand a year. His finger nails would never be clean and he was too old to learn the difference between a cuspidor and a rug. He was wide and square and his left shoulder sagged under the burden of a muscle that had hammered red-hot iron for twenty years and wrestled with the hindlegs of nervous mules. His cheek bulged with star plug and his wide red face beamed with anticipation. . . . Ladies would never like him but men knew what he was worth.

Eusebio Gonzales was there, too—a smooth brown plump young Mexican with a black moustache and a small twinkling eye. He looked like the jolliest man alive and he was. In his jolly way he had shot seven men, had five times been tried for homicide and each time acquitted by a jury which unanimously held that the fight had been fair and the other fellow was out of luck. Eusebio was now the most successful criminal lawyer in the town with an almost unbroken record for winning acquittals from native juries. Jurors seemed reluctant to disagree with him. Eusebio was a deadly enemy and a warm friend and had never been

[169]

known to back water. He was a necessary member of the Kelly Club. So was Sol Rosenberg, whose name was a monument in this far place to the ubiquity of the chosen people. He had started in business with a burro load of trinkets, cheap jewelry and religious images for the native trade. Forever would follow him his celebrated pronouncement when his burro rolled off a trail and smashed the stock. "There's Christ and Saint Peter and the Pope all gone to Hell!" His tiny store in Old Town had fattened on the railroad trade. He had begun buying wool and formed valuable connections in Boston. He was hailed with a chorus of Hello Solly. Tom Foote once voiced the general feeling about him. "Sol may be a sheeny but he sure is a white one."

Here men met in the warm solidarity of a struggle shared, in a fraternity that laid aside prejudice and asked of each man only that he pay his debts, keep his nerve, and tend to his own business.

The guests to-night included several distinguished strangers—a young Englishman touring the West, a United States senator stumping the country for the Republicans, a scientist from the Smithsonian Institute who was studying the problem of rainfall and had sent up explosive balloons in a fruitless effort to break the drought, a large mysterious person whose mutton chop whiskers had started a rumor that he was a New York capitalist. He had already been offered many bargains in mining stock and desert land. These were introduced all around, their hands were crippled in a crushing cordiality and they were herded onto the little platform embowered in bunting. They were the guests of honor, the victims in chief. Each of them would have to loosen up before the night was over.

Tom Foote was president of the Kelly Club and he rose now to make the opening speech. Robert, and all others who knew Tom well, could tell by the solemn dignity of his bearing that he had refreshed himself for this effort with several of his favorite sloe gin rickies. Up to a certain point liquor always made Tom more dignified, more fluent and grammatical—though his grammar was never a thing you could count on.

Tom was one old-timer who had kept up with the band wagon. Despite his heavy investments in the liquor business his social position was secure. This was partly because all women liked him but also partly because he moved with the times. He was one of the first to buy a dress suit just as he had done more than any other one man to jam the railroad bill through the legislature against the Mexican opposition. He was a booster for the library fund and a member of the school board. He had brushed the alkali dust out of his hair, transferred his gun from his belt to his pocket, put on a hard hat and a high collar and with amaz-

ing success had applied to political and social purposes an eloquence schooled in the hard persuasion
of reluctant mules. . . . His face was a bright red
and his dress collar had collapsed in the struggle
with his hot and restless neck but his deportment
was as perfect as that of a preacher at a funeral.

"Gentlemen," he began. "Most of those here
present is familiar with this Club and its activities
but for the benefit of the strangers in our midst I
will say that the Kelly Club is a moral and educa-
tional institution. Its purposes as stated in the con-
stitution and by-laws, is to put down liquor and
hold badger fights. The putting down of liquor
to-night will be left for each and everyone to do
as he thinks fit and let his conscience be his guide,
but we are all gathered together for the purpose
of holding a badger fight and for the benefit of
the distinguished strangers in our midst, who may
never have seen a badger fight, I will say that the
New Mexico badger is the fightinest thing of its
size that walks the earth. Jest to see this little
animal in action is a liberal education for young
and old. If a badger was as big as a grizzly ba'r a
buzz-saw wouldn't be no match for him. . . . Now
gentlemen under that there little wooden box is
concealed a large male badger which has never
tasted defeat. His opponent in to-night's little
shindy will be that large white bull dog which the
boy is holding over there in the corner. That there

[172]

dog has licked every other dog he has ever gone up against and the question now is, can he whip this badger, and I am told that the odds at present is five to three in favor of the badger.

"Now Gentlemen, it is always customary at these events to let some distinguished guest of the Club lift the box off the badger which is the signal that starts the fight. This honor by unanimous agreement of the committee in charge has been conferred to-night on the Honorable (at this point Tom consulted notes) Henry Alfred Fitzwilliam-Jones of London, England, who is touring this country with a view to the possible purchase of ranch properties and of settling in our midst. . . . Gentlemen, Mr. Fitzwilliam-Jones!"

A stocky blond young man, his face fiery with new sunburn and embarrassment, wearing a heavy coarse woolen suit and huge square-toed tan shoes, rose, grinned, bowed, backed into his chair and sat down again while the crowd clapped, stamped and whistled through its teeth.

Tom went over to the visitor, took him by the arm, all but lifted him out of his chair, conducted him to the badger-concealing box, placed a little string in his hand and whispered instructions in his ear. Then he raised a hand for silence.

"At the count of three," he announced. "The badger and the bulldog will both be turned loose and Mr. Fitzwilliam-Jones will get one of the big surprises of his life."

He counted, the young Briton pulled and stood staring open-mouthed at empty floor.

The crowd poured down on him, yelling like hounds on cornered game. He was pushed and thrown this way and that. The scarlet of his face deepened almost to purple. For an awful moment it looked as though the joke might not penetrate the British consciousness—as though he might lash out with his great square fists. But a large white grin finally broke through the dark perplexity of his countenance.

The badgering was over.

The victim was slapped on the back, patted on the head, shaken by the hand. To a thunder of applause he was endorsed as a good fellow and nominated as an honorary member of the Kelly Club.

When the rumpus had died down Tom took the floor again.

"Now gentlemen," he said. "The chief sporting event of the evening is over and we will proceed to more serious matters. We have in our midst to-night one of the most learned gentlemen that has ever been seen in these parts—Professor Amos J. McGavock of the Smithsonian Institution, Washington, D. C. Professor McGavock is a meteorologist, which name, in ordinary language, means a weather man. The Professor can tell you what the weather is going to be to-morrow, at least sometimes he can, for all of us is liable to err, and he can tell you why it rains when it does rain and why it don't rain when it don't. Now this whole subject is of the foremost importance to this great growing empire of the Southwest. Just a few years ago someone said that all we needed out here to make it a great country was water and good society. Now since the railroad come, bringing with it some of the fairest flowers of pure womanhood that ever bloomed, and such distinguished visitors as we have in our midst to-night, we have been getting good society in bunches, but we still need water the worst way. This fact is most painfully impressed on all of us right now when we ain't had a drop of rain for over a month and the sheep ranges is burning up and the river is getting so low a frog can hardly keep his hide wet. One good heavy shower right now would be worth half a million dollars in the pockets of the merchants of this town.

"Now Professor McGavock come all the way out here for no other purpose than to give us this percipitation which we so badly need. He done all that modern science knows how to make it rain. He sent up balloons which was designed to bust the clouds wide open and let down the water. For reasons which is in the keeping of an inscrutable Providence, nothing dropped. Either the clouds was too high or the balloons wasn't strong enough or something. The important point is that this learned man come to us in our hour of need and done all that he could for us. The Professor's faith in science is more than proved, to my way of thinking, by the fact that he brought with him and carried every day a fine large umbarella, which he never had no occasion to use. In this country, where umbarellas is as scarce as earmuffs in hell, it seems to me the Professor's umbarella ought to be an inspiration to us all. It is my earnest hope and my firm belief that the Professor may yet see water fall in this thirsty land. . . . Now gentlemen the Professor will speak a few words on this important subject of rain and how to make it fall and I am sure he will have the undivided attention of everybody. . . . Gentlemen, Professor McGavock!"

The Professor was a short stout man, red with heat as was everyone else in the hall, visibly shy and embarrassed, wholly in earnest. He bowed stiffly before a storm of applause and lifted up a small serious voice against the hush that followed.

"Gentlemen," he began. "The thing to remember about this problem of precipitation in arid areas is that moisture in gaseous form is nearly always present at certain more or less ascertainable elevations above the surface of the earth. The problem therefore is one of condensation. In a word, while we cannot make water, we may be able to make it fall.''

The Professor paused and during the pause Tom was seen to rise halfway out of his seat and make frantic gestures, as though to a hidden presence above the Professor's head among the decorations. The presence materialized for the eyes of acute observers as a small boy lying along a plank hidden among the bunting and some could see the artfully concealed bucket which he now upended so that its contents descended full upon the bald perspiring head of Professor McGavock.

The change wrought in his countenance was all that the most exacting practitioner of the primitive of art of practical jokery could have wished. The Professor was literally struck dumb, his mouth wide open for utterance, one hand raised in a nascent gesture. So he stood for fully a minute while the wool house quivered under a thunderclap of mirth. . . .

Chapter Five

FOUR o'clock in the morning and he was going home.

He wasn't drunk and he didn't intend for any-one who might see him to think he was drunk. He never got drunk. When the occasion called for it he would take a drink with his friends but he never got drunk. If anyone saw him now they would see a prominent citizen in a dress suit walking home late and alone from a convivial gathering and walking with the utmost dignity. He carried his hat in his hand because his brow was a little overheated and he held himself to a strict and perhaps slightly exaggerated perpendicular.

Railroad Avenue was still alive with lights and men. He could see several he knew for whom the whole sidewalk wasn't wide enough. A fellow just ahead of him was weaving from one side of it to the other, always in danger of plunging over the four foot precipice into the street.

In order to make sure that he was not wavering himself Robert laid his course by a telegraph pole. He was going straight toward it, no doubt of that, but the sidewalk seemed sometimes to bulge under his feet and sometimes to fall away.

He passed three drunken Mexicans making their way along the wall of Rosenberg's Big Red Store like blind men and singing as they went, a sad and reedy ballad. Two men on horses came by in a dead run waving in their saddles like grass in the wind. . . . Funny how a drunk will never fall off a horse. A man in liquor can ride better than he can walk. . . . The last street car bound for Old Town carried a lusty chorus of male voices on the rear platform. Every block it pulled up and took on a few more, some of whom had to be lifted. . . . Well it was the biggest night in the history of the town and it deserved to be celebrated and everything was all right. There hadn't been a single shot fired except in fun and not even a fist fight worth mentioning. . . . This town was civilized . . . law'n' order . . . homes and churches . . . wives and children . . . Emily! Gentlemen, this is my wife. . . . Why hadn't he said something or done something? Paralyzed tongue-tied idiot! It seemed so easy now. Take her by the hand. . . . A woman just like a horse you have to touch. . . . Talk alone no good. . . . How they act under your hand. . . . It always took a few drinks to make him sociable. . . .

He was conscious of this as one of many nights of wine that had broken barriers and brought him close to men and women. Without liquor it seemed to him he would never have found friends or

[179]

lovers. Something like that it took to crack his shell.

He had never felt so much a part of the bunch as to-night at the Kelly Club and after when he and Tom and Sol and Diego and three or four others had gone down to Tom's place. . . . Finest saloon in the Southwest with a solid mahogany bar, a brass rail and lights shining on polished glasses and mirrors and a magnificent oil painting of dancing nymphs on the back wall. The brass spittoons alone cost fifteen dollars apiece. Tom doing the honors. "Keep your money in your pockets boys. It won't buy anything to-night." Tom's heavy hand on his shoulder. "Gentlemen I propose the health of a man that's done more than any other to make this town what it is to-day, the best friend and the squarest partner that ever lived. When he and I started in business back in the sixties we didn't have nothing but our nerve and more'n once we come damn near losing that. We starved together and froze together and went in the hole together and crawled out together. Leastways Bob here crawled out and pulled me after him. But for his head for figgers I wouldn't be where I am to-night. Gentlemen, I give you the good health of Bob Jayson. Here's to lead in his pencil and jack in his jeans!"

Afterwards down the street they went in a long row, arms around shoulders, fuller than ever, bellowing songs—railroad versions. "The sonuvabitch jumped over the fence. Goodby my lover goodby."

Down the line they went as a matter of course. Everybody was headed that way. This street of painted ladies was the town's real wife and sweetheart. To men riding in from long months at mines and ranches or prospecting this was a fountain of love in the desert. . . . A bath, a shave and a haircut and then down to Grace's or Mollie's or Joe's. . . . And nearly everybody in town was there on Saturday night and on nights of celebration such as this.

Grace herself flung the door open to them.

"Come in, old timers, come in! I notice wherever else you go you always end up here!"

She was beautiful, too, in spite of her paint and her hair bleached to the color of a new rope and fluffed out big as a tumbleweed. Her arms were magnificent, braceleted in gold and diamonds, and her large handsome white hands were heavy with rings that commemorated conquest like notches on a killer's gun. . . . The little girl that tried to climb in his lap when he first came to town! She slapped him on the back.

"As I live, old Bobby Jayson, the boy with the stiff neck. . . . This *IS* a big night. . . . We're gonna have a drink on the house boys. Name your poison! . . . Come on in, girls. Here's the big red store and the new saloon and the first national bank and the water works!"

In came the picked beauties imported from the Gold Coast, ravishing the eyes of men with naked arms and shoulders. The celebrated maid with the lace top-knot came in bearing drinks on a tray and the Professor sat down to the piano and played "After the Ball was over." This was gilded vice for you! This was a sporting house for gentlemen!

Soon most were up and dancing, Sol Rosenberg grinning like a possum in the conquering arms of Grace, murmuring in her ear dubious but effective gallantries so that she threw back her head and hurled at the ceiling her great shattering laugh, hard as a battle shout and as full of fighting energy.

Robert who alone sat in a corner, tapping a foot, watched her with amazed fascination.

A girl came weaving across the room and sat on his lap without so much as by your leave. She was young and her face was a painted image of half-witted lust with no brow at all and great warm eyes and a red wound of painted mouth that menaced his own. To escape her he lifted her off his knee and danced, but she wrapped herself around him and stuck to him like poison ivy to a tree. He looked around wildly for ways of escape, wholly averse in his mind while his body treasonously warmed to her sinuous assault. . . .

Over by the stairway a row had started. Tom

Foote and Jim Hepburn, who had just come in, faced each other with clenched fists, Tom red and aggressive, the handsome thin young Englishman pale and scared but giving no ground. Grace pushed between them, seized Tom by the lapels and backed him into a corner.

"No you don't, you big stiff. . . . I won't have no rough stuff in my house and I go upstairs with whoever I damn please."

The party was wrecked. Robert and Sol Rosenberg and Diego closed in on Tom, half dragged and half persuaded him out the door. In the cool night air he sobered. As he and Robert walked away together he became morosely sentimental. It was only in a certain stage of liquor that he ever talked of Grace.

"I always swear I won't go near that place and as sure as I take three drinks I always do. . . . I can't get over it, Bob. When she was eighteen she was the spittin' image of my mother. . . . I offered to marry her before she got in that trouble and I went to 'Frisco and offered to marry her after, and she told me to go to hell and I ain't never laid a hand on her to this day . . ." He stopped and turned to Robert and laid a hand on his shoulder, looked at him with a calf-eyed wistfulness that went grotesquely with his mighty frame and the red crag of his face.

"Y'know what she said to me once, Bob. . . . And

I ain't never told this to a living soul. . . . She said she wouldn't never let me touch her because if she did she'd go soft and she didn't want to never go soft on nobody. . . . God, ain't it hell!"

He had taken Tom home and then set out alone on foot, refusing lifts, feeling that fresh air and exercise would do him good. A little queazy in the middle and his mind a tossing confusion of images when he started, he felt much better by the time he reached the stretch of lonely road between Old Town and New.

Until he came to the cornfields and orchards along the main ditch it was all weed and brush with scattered patches of tall sunflowers. In the light of half a moon he saw jackrabbits run across the road and crickets made a steady soothing music.

Dry open country under a clear sky always made him feel better, bringing many faint memories of peaceful nights on the road scattered over twenty years. . . . The road he once had hated and had come to love. He had always been glad to get out of the store and take the road again. He carried a picture in his mind of every waterhole between the Cimarron and the Missouri. He could think of any one of them and remember nights when he had lain on the ground smoking a last pipe, feeling that inexplicable peacefulness that seems to come up from the earth and down from the sky. All the old timers knew it and none of the newcomers understood. . . . The road that had shortened year by year as the dream of rails came true, the road that had died that day!

It made him feel old to remember so far back and such different things and yet young he felt too. He had not cracked or softened. He had never known such a zest for doing things as now, nor had so many things to do. . . . To-morrow to the sawmill and then Wednesday night with luck at Socorro to see if the stampmill had come and try to pull Eli Hughes out of trouble and send him out into the Mogollons. . . . Only in the wilderness was Eli safe. . . . Back Sunday and call on her and take her for a drive. . . . He had his life planned and felt competent to live it. Only there was so little time. Days that once had been so long flew by with a speed that frightened, like when he first rode on a train and saw trees and telegraph poles dash past the car window.

Not in years had he come home so late. He went in as quietly as he could. The old woman would be scandalized if she knew and the worst of it was she would wake him at seven the same as ever. With no matches left in his pockets he fumbled a long time before he found one and lit a lamp, making several passes at the wick before he succeeded. His hand was unsteady but his head was clear. Never had past and future run such a bright stream through his mind as now when he sat down to take off dusty shoes for silence sake. . . . Never had he been so conscious of the marvel of his destiny—he, Robert Jayson, starting way back there green and poor and now, look! He stood up in his sock feet, tremendously conscious of his dignity and power, fumbling at his little white bow tie and oddly unable to get it undone.

Mrs. Latz creaked a door open and stuck out her head, emergent on a scrawney red neck from a voluminous blue wrapper, her gray hair done tightly in curl papers, like an aged Medusa whose serpents had shrivelled and died. Her expression at first was one of blinking surprised severity but she discovered some comic aspect in the situation of which he was wholly unconscious. She threw back her head in a high shrill cackle of mirth.

"You look so fonny," she gasped. "So red in the face, joost like a turkey gobbler angry. . . . You should be ashamed . . . at your age. . . . *Aber wass* is the matter. Can you *nicht* undo it. . . . Come, I help you."

She bundled calico about her, flapped her carpet slippers across the floor and undid the tie with a single twitch of dexterous bony fingers.

"Can you all right do it now *oder* do you want I should put you in bed like a great big baby!"

While she spoke he was painfully aware of Annie, seen in a narrow space of opened door as a great cloud of brown hair, large soft sleepy eyes and a white round young arm and hand clutching pink fluffiness. Mrs. Latz chuckled again when he refused further aid and still chuckling flapped back into her room, leaving him facing Annie with a feeling of irritated embarrassment.

Annie should quickly have closed her door but instead she smiled, gathered at once with a curiously quick graceful movement her skirts and her body, pranced across the floor on slim bare feet and planted on his lips a quick shy kiss. Then she turned and ran back into her room and closed the door without looking back.

He stood staring at the closed door with the vacancy of mind and absence of impulse which follows sharp surprise. . . . Why, he asked himself deliberately, had Annie felt called upon to kiss him? Why, he asked himself again, shouldn't Annie kiss him? Hadn't he known her from the age of eleven, held her on his knee, given her candy, sent her to school? . . . Annie had kissed him good-by when she went away. . . . But not before since she came back. And this was nothing like that. Annie's kiss had changed too. . . . Pity he had seen in her eyes and he didn't like it. She had felt impelled to comfort him because she saw the old woman made him feel foolish. That was like Annie. Yes but that was not all. No by golly that was not all!

In a high state of confusion, of inexplicable ela-

tion, he went to his own room. As he got himself
fumblingly out of his togs his brow wrinkled with
a perplexity he did not feel quite competent just
then to analyze. Several times he paused to wipe
his mouth firmly with the back of his hand and
with each gesture he pushed Annie resolutely a
little farther out of his mind.

Chapter Six

Iɴ a light buckboard behind tall shiny bays he rocked and swayed along a sandy road in a white glare of sun that made him squint and warmed his back like a fire.

To him it was a discomfort so familiar that he liked it. He rested his eyes on a purple wall of mesa, gripped a cigar between his teeth and let himself roll with the road. But he never completely relaxed. Every time the team slowed in heavy sand he slapped the laboring rumps with the reins and chirruped. He drove hard in spite of himself and his resolutions not to. He used up horses. A team never lasted him long. The nervous rush of his energy poured into them and burned them out. He was always in a hurry to get where he was going. He never had enough time.

He had found everything all right at the mill. A satisfying picture of it lingered in his mind. . . . Yellow fragrant sawdust piled up into a little mountain beside an unpainted frame building that trembled as in rage and screamed with the hoarse voice of a buzz saw tearing its way through four foot pine logs. . . . His men were cutting timber far up on the mountainside now. Standing beside

[189]

the mill he had seen the great green tops sway to the whang of axes, heard the crashing fall of a hundred feet of timber, the roar of logs skidding to the canyon bottom, the shouts of teamsters hauling them to the saw.

The canyon all around the mill was a stripped and ravished thing. In the spring it had been the prettiest stand of yellow pine he ever saw with nearly every tree a hundred feet high or better and the ground brown and slippery with needles centuries deep. He had always liked pine timber best of all—fragrant time-defying forest where storm turned into music and sunlight splintered into living patterns. It shocked him a little to see this one reduced to stumps and smoking piles of top-brush and the ground torn to dust by heavy-loaded wheels. But if he hadn't done it someone else would have. He had been lucky to get there first. Likely as not it would have burned if it hadn't been cut. There were forest fires all over the mountains ever since the railroad came. Some said the Utes set them to spite the whites but the camp fires of prospectors and settlers were probably as much to blame as anything else. Men were overrunning the country, eating it up. But you couldn't stop progress and after all it was a big country and there seemed to be more than enough of everything for everybody.

While he was at the mill a man drove in with

a wagon load of deer and he bought venison for his men at five cents a pound when beef was twenty. Professional hunters worked out the canyons systematically, killed bucks, does, fawns—everything. . . . When his workmen wanted trout they threw a stick of dynamite into a pool. It blew up a great shattering silver spurt of water and hundreds of dead fish rained down. More than half of them were wasted and he didn't like that, but it was no use trying to stop such things. The country had to develop. Timber was to cut, game and fish were to eat. . . . A little band of Mescalero Apaches rode into camp that evening—dirty ragged lousy wretches on lean sorebacked ponies. They had left their reservation to hunt and had nearly starved to death. They said all the game was gone. They begged scraps at the cook shack and when they saw the carcass of a mule that had broken a leg and been shot they asked for it. Robert watched them butcher the thing, squabbling with bloody knives in their hands over the best pieces, but when the women and children began pulling out little fat entrails and chewing them up like sticks of licorice he had to turn away. . . . Indians were out of luck these days. It was hard to realize that just a few years ago they had owned the country, all but a few settlements and guarded roads. Smart men then believed they would never let the railroad through. Daniel Webster wanted to give them the West and

[191]

get out and back in the sixties the Secretary of War recommended withdrawing all troops. All at once they had gone to pieces and more on liquor, smallpox and syphilis than anything else. People never would know what Indians had been like. . . . He remembered the swoop and yell of painted warriors—remembered what he would never remember without a twitch of pain. But he no longer hated Indians. The Indians he hated all were dead and what remained were a few drunken beggars.

He had given his last instructions to Gorley, his foreman at the mill, the night before so that he could be on the road at daybreak. Everything would go along just the same without him. He merely put in an appearance once in a while for the sake of discipline.

With some difficulty he had learned how to look stern, kick and threaten, make men think they might lose their jobs. He could see things speed up wherever he went and he could gauge nicely just about how often it was necessary to put on the pressure of his presence. . . . Money made some men conceited but he had never gotten over the lucky wonder of his success. . . . How easy it was to make men work for you if you had a little money! He got the contract for lumber and bought the timber on the stump and now nearly a hundred men sweated at a few dollars a day to make him rich. He could neither cut a tree or run a mill but he was turning out thousands of board feet a day at a fifty percent profit. Gorley was a man he admired, one who could make men and mules work. Robert had seen him mend a broken piston rod and throw a large drunken Irishman into a waterhole the same morning and think nothing of it. Gorley could do anything but save money and so he owned Gorley.

Save money and wait—that was all he had done. . . . It seemed such a little while ago that he and Tom were batching in the room behind the store, cooking their own beans and chile and eggs —whatever the day's trade brought in. Some days when it brought in neither cash nor chuck they would take an old muzzle-loading shotgun Tom had, go down into the wet alkaline pastures by the river and shoot the wild-fowl that streamed across the red flare of the sunset. On the way home in early fall they would sometimes climb over a fence and lift a few bunches of grapes or a late melon for dessert. With these and a quart of native wine worth about fifteen cents they would dine in style.

Those were lean days but not bad ones, not by a damn sight. He liked to turn them over and over in his mind. . . . They went to all the fiestas in those days—Dia San Juan and Dia San Felipe and all the rest—where the young Mexicans played *gallo,* stooping from their running ponies to snatch at the head of a rooster buried in the sand. Tom played with them and Robert himself joined in games of shinny, one whole town against another battling over a wooden block in a cloud of dust. They never missed a dance or a horse race and they had a spotted pony named Pinto that could beat anything for a quarter of a mile. Pinto did much to keep the firm solvent for a year or two.

They used to sit in the store playing coon-can and bet how long it would be until a customer came and when one did, more often than not it would be Tom's girl or his, come to beg a pound of coffee or a handful of chile.

Long lazy days of *poco tiempo* before he learned to hurry, before he felt the sting of moneylust. . . . Slowly their business had grown until they had six wagons on the road. Then came the awful day, the day he could never bear to remember. Half their stock went up in the flame he watched that haunted night and he rode home from his one Indian battle, half crazy, wavering in his saddle, to face debt and the panic of seventy-three on top of it.

Those were days he got through painfully by inches like a man walking on blistered feet and there were nights when he woke up and looked hungrily down the muzzle of a gun. . . . Yet that was the one time in all his life when he had felt conscious of triumph. Tom wanted to sell out, di-

vide the money among their creditors and quit.
Tom wanted to go gold hunting in Colorado. Robert wanted to stick and did stick with a stubborn-
ness he never himself understood. He couldn't buy
Tom out and nobody else would, so Tom had to
stick. They quarreled, they cursed each other, they
would have fought except that Tom wouldn't hit
a man smaller than himself. Robert covered many
sheets with figures to prove they could work out of
the hole and Tom wouldn't even look at the figures.
Robert talked railroad until Tom reached for
something to throw every time he heard the word.
The railroad was crossing Kansas then but few believed it would come down the Rio Grande in less
than a hundred years. Don Aragon was working
against it in the legislature on the ground that it
would ruin the wagon trade and throw half the
population out of work, and he had all the Mexicans solid against it. The priests in the churches
were telling the people the railroad would mean
giving the country to gringoes and infidels.

Then came the change, sooner and greater than
anyone could have expected. Eastern money greased
the way through the legislature and cocked Winchesters settled the fight for Raton Pass. Years
before the railroad reached it, railroad money had
transformed the town. They blew the dust off
goods that had lain on the shelf for years and
sold them for three times what they had cost. Land

they had taken reluctantly for bad debts suddenly turned into golden coin.

For years they had kept the company assets in a little canvas sack that he tossed on top of an old wardrobe every night and climbed up on a chair to get every morning. Three years before the railroad came they had to haul in a great iron safe with the firm name painted on the door.

That safe he remembered as he did some persons who made changes in his life. Big and square it stood behind him and pushed. . . . The money in it made him go. It was like a woman that stays behind in a room, yet moves a man wherever he is. He liked to turn the combination, swing the great door and take out money that would bind men and drive them, cut timber and make dirt fly. He was dazzled by it at first like a kid with a new toy. It became a familiar thing, but he never lost the thrill of wielding money, of seeing money grow. . . . So many new things there were to do with money in a changing country. And then, on top of it all, little Eli and the silver mine. . . . They had named it the Long Shot. . . .

Chapter Seven

IT was near dusk when he topped the hills west of the valley and drove down the long sandy slope towards Socorro. His fagged team plodded in heavy sand, their rumps and flanks streaked with sweat and caked with dust. His destination in sight he was content to take it easy and rest a moment in the cooling air and softening tone of evening.

At this hour the glare died suddenly. Shadows ran down the hills and filled the arroyos. Dust touched by slanting light hung in frail nebular beauty above the valley roads and the river was a thin bright streak, spent in its struggle with heat and sand. . . . When the sun dropped and the evening breeze came up every man that rode across the mesas felt at once lifted and soothed.

For a little while he gave way to this familiar mood, watched a soaring buzzard make slow circles in the sky, followed the far course of a frightened jack-rabbit.

But little Eli was on his mind. . . . Not that Eli was any special responsibility of his, but a stray dog that followed him could always get his attention. He had a conscience that hunted trouble. He took no pride in it. He had helped enough people in his life to learn how thankless and generally how useless a job it was. . . . He had staked Eli again and again just because he didn't have the guts to turn away a man hungry and broke. Eli could have gotten jobs but he was one of those prospectors that have the bug and can't do anything else. He was one that could punch a burro across mountains alone for six months at a stretch. Fellows like that learned to live on next to nothing. Ten pounds of beans and a side of bacon would last them as long as it would a mouse. They killed game and caught fish and sponged on sheep outfits and cattle camps where no man was ever refused a meal. They learned to do without everything— women, comfort, talk—everything but their freedom. He could understand Eli in a way. Any man could who had lived in the country long enough to get the feel of it. . . . You came in from a trip burned and thirsty and saddle-sore and swore you were done, and in a week you wanted to go again . . . that go-again feeling. . . . He had it himself. It was Eli's whole life till he got that chunk of money, and then everything else in him bubbled up. . . . He ran wild on liquor and women. The money was too much and too sudden, for him as for a good many others. Some men it made and some it killed as sure as gunshot. All it changed.

It had changed Eli more than anyone would have

believed possible. A small wiry bald man with pale
eyebrows that hardly showed and brown smooth
skin, he somehow suggested one of those Mexican
hairless dogs. He had a timid manner and a small
quiet voice. He was never dirty but always dusty
as though he just crawled up out of the sand. If
you gave him a drink he would take it and sip it
about an hour. He was used to making things last.

He wouldn't look at a woman any more than if
she wasn't there. Those fellows often lost all feeling for women—sexless and ageless they seemed—
those fellows who turned their backs on the towns
and lost everything but freedom. Eli looked sometimes like a big overgrown baby and other times
as old as the hills. But he couldn't have been so old
—probably not much past forty—or he couldn't
have blossomed out the way he did. He raised a
surprising red moustache that changed the whole
look of his face, hiding his childish bewildered
mouth. In a big white bucket of a hat and a new
blue suit and tan boots he was another man. He
had a good build and small feet and the big pearl-
handled Colt he carried seemed to make him feel
deadly and invulnerable.

Then he got hold of that woman, or she got
hold of him. She was a waitress in one of the
miners' boarding houses and probably made a little
money on the side the same as all the rest of them.
But after she became Eli's girl nobody could look

[199]

at her, much less chuck her under the chin. He wanted her treated like Queen Victoria. He flashed his gun three or four times and made several good men back water, partly because nobody expected him to show fight. Then he shot a miner—beat him to the draw fair enough—and after that he went on a rampage, rode his horse into a store, shot out a few windows.

It was then that McMasters sent word to Robert to come and get Eli. They couldn't do anything with him. . . . Socorro, like all other tough towns, was safe as a church for anyone who minded his own business. You didn't need to pack a gun. The fighting was all among a lot of men that wanted to fight for the fun of it. It was a sport and a social diversion that started in the track-end towns in the sixties and spread to all the mining camps. There was always some bad man who claimed to be running the town and some other fellow was going to bust him loose from his bottom the first time he got funny. In due course they were both buried without prayer.

They had averaged a killing a week in Socorro for a long time but only a few indictments had been returned. Everybody was too busy making money to take much interest in private quarrels. If it was a fair fight it was all right. But shooting up the town was another matter. It wasn't appreciated— especially if there was any property damage. Glass windows and bar fixtures cost money and peaceful citizens didn't like stray bullets zipping around. A man might do it once and get away with a warning, but if he tried it again, he had to be a good man to live. A Billy the Kid could ride into a town and own it but not an Eli Hughes.

Eli had pushed himself into the dangerous society of the gunmen. He had made himself a nuisance at least once. He had taken on a part he wasn't equal to. . . . It was necessary for Eli's health that he go for a long trip in the hills.

Robert drove into the edge of town about dark, put up his team at Garney's livery stable and started on foot for the plaza in search of supper and of Eli.

The heart of the town reached his senses from afar as a glow of light looming over black square adobe outlines, a jangle of cheap pianos and a vague chorus of human excitement that grew in volume as he neared it, became articulate in high shrill laughter, deep guffaws and shouted words.

Approaching it wearily and without eagerness he yet was aware of a faint thrill, a stir and hum of the blood, as though the air were filled with an orgiastic tremor no human flesh could fail to feel.

Just two years before the town had been a perfect piece of the old-time Mexican life—of sun-soaked adobe, deep shade and sleepy quiet, like his own town when he first went there. . . . An atmosphere he knew and loved . . . lazy, quiet, but with a note of music about it, a throb of passion, a hidden streak of red . . . a life of indolent men who yet could fight, of sleepy women waiting for night and lovers . . . a life of ancient tunes and games, moving untroubled in folkways too old to question. . . . He knew that life had given him something he needed, set something in him free. To see a bit of it shattered and overwhelmed, as here it was, made him feel sorry for a minute. . . . But the glare and racket of the plaza drew him. He was a part of that noise. He had his fingers in the silver too, and his whole being tingled to the touch.

Every building on the plaza now, except the bank, was a combination saloon, dance hall and gambling joint. Some of the old adobes had been converted to the purpose and some of them had been torn down to make way for flimsy wooden buildings with enormous signs over their doors. Yellow lamplight lit the square and flickered to the restless rhythm of swinging doors that showed glimpses of crowded bars, of eager knots around faro and monte tables and of floors where lumbering heavy-footed men capered and shouted, clutching short-skirted bare-shouldered girls with painted faces and mouths as hard as a crack in a rock. . . . It took underground miners to make a town wild.

There were few Mexicans here now—more

Irish and Yankee than anything else with a sprinkling of Welch and English and some great blond Scandinavians. Nearly all were big men, some short and stocky but with enormous shoulders. It was a town of giants and gnomes let loose from under the earth, running amock. They were skilled and highly paid men who followed the big strikes of silver and gold, went down into the earth wherever the money was, worked ten and twelve hours a day furiously in dark and damp, risking fire, cave-in and tunnel gas, then came surging up all at once in the evening, mad for light, release, excitement, for music, warmth and women. Great drunken rollicking children, they went about shouting, laughing, quarreling, throwing money away on crooked games. . . . And among them everywhere moved tightlipped men and women, whores and gamblers, with cunning eyes and hidden weapons, greedily raking money across tables, stuffing money into stockings and pockets, watching, careful under cover of a frantic fake delight, wary of sudden violence and rage.

Robert went into Curley's, the biggest joint in town, ordered a drink and watched the crowd for Eli or for someone who might have seen him. On one side of the room about fifty men squared up to a bar, rattled money on it and lifted drinks. The mirror behind it was a shifting picture of faces in every stage of liquor from beaming garrulous good humor to wobbling imbecility with eyes that rolled out of focus and mouths that dribbled and mumbled. A door at the back showed glimpses of a crowded dance floor and along the other wall were games—two poker tables with alert bouncers and watchers standing over the players to keep some kind of order and collect the kitty for the house, a keeno game with about forty men buying cards, and a roulette layout with a woman spinning the wheel and a crowd staring at her and at the table. She was a woman of real beauty, with clear-cut features, her eyelids painted black and her cheeks carmine. She wore a velvet gown cut to the crotch of her breasts and her bare white arms were bound in gold and diamonds. Robert had heard of her— Kate Dougall, Jim Curley's girl. It was said she cleaned up thousands a week and largely because the miners could not resist her looks. Robert saw a great red-faced fellow, visibly tipsy, sidle closer and closer to her, finally reach out a great muscular stubby hand and touch her white arm as a child might touch some bright irresistible trinket. She turned on him with a queenly look of haughty reproof. A bouncer got him by the front of the shirt and began to back him toward the door. He protested, explained, lost his temper and raised a great square fist to strike. Instantly he was buried under four men and hustled out the door before the crowd knew anything had happened.

Robert finally found Eli in a small saloon across the plaza. Expansively drunk, with his great hat pushed back from his red bald brow, he was holding forth to a small group of grinning miners. He wore his pearl-handled Colt conspicuously on his right hip with the tip of the holster tied to his leg after the most approved fashion for man-killers. Without hearing a word Robert felt sure that Eli was telling what he was going to do to somebody and the others were egging him on. . . . When he saw Robert he seemed to forget all the others. He came forward holding out his hand.

"Bob, old head, I'm glad to see you. Have a drink!"

Robert got him by the arm and lead him easily away.

"Not right now, Eli. I want to have a talk with you . . . got a proposition . . . need your help. Come on over to Garney's. We can talk in his office."

"No, you come up to Emma's with me. I promised to be there at eight and it's nine now. . . . I got her fixed up fine. I want you to meet her and I want to tell you about this little trouble I'm in. Y'know that low-lived bastard, Joe Fowler? Well, he said something about Emma I can't stand for. Three or four told me. I been looking for him all evening. He's keeping out of my way . . ."

"Forget it, Eli! Forget it! You can't spend your

life hunting every damn fool that gets drunk and says something dirty. I've got something else for you to do. McMasters and I want you to go out and hunt where the vein crops out on the other side of the Magdalenas. You know you said yourself it must come out over there somewhere and you're the boy that can find it if anybody can."

"All right Bob, all right. Just as soon as I settle with that pig-loving sonuvabitch. . . . I don't want to go nowhere but I'd go anywhere for you."

"There's no time to lose, Eli. Somebody else'll get onto it."

"We ain't gonna lose no time, Bob. It won't take me five minutes to settle that pie-eyed pup oncet I get my sights on him."

Talking excitedly, he led the way to a door and knocked.

Emma was a surprise to Robert. He had expected a typical open-town floosey with hard money-hunting eyes. He saw a thin blond girl, a little taller than Eli. Her almost colorless hair was fluffed and curled and her mouth was somewhat amateurishly painted. But it was not the mouth of a prostitute—that unmistakable mouth of sensuality hardened into a weapon. It was a soft weak mouth and the expression of her large pale eyes was a wholly timid one. It struck Robert that what Eli had found was not so much a temptress as something to pity and protect.

Emma wore a gown of yellow silk, grotesquely ill-fitting and enormous of skirt, but happily chosen as to color. She brought out a bottle of wine and some cup cakes and played the part of a shy but not ungraceful hostess. An unattractive woman, thin and colorless, Robert thought her at first, but as she moved about the room he became aware of a sensuous appeal in the swing of her hips and the turn of her ankle, and also of a thin timid charm in her laugh.

He got in a few polite questions and learned that she was from Texas and a widow. She had started for California with her husband in a wagon, he had died in El Paso and she found a job in a miners' boarding house. . . . So much he learned, but he could not understand either the woman or her relation to Eli. Both were so different from what he had expected. . . . The way the two looked at each other and laughed—giggled was the word —and the way she dropped her eyes and blushed a perfectly genuine blush that tinted even her thin neck. They seemed almost adolescent, grotesquely and touchingly young. And she must have been well past thirty.

Robert took up his argument again. Eli must go at once—for purely business reasons.

"You can take Mrs. Gower here with you. You say you're going to be married right away. There's a shack in Magdalena where you two can keep house first rate."

The woman gulped a deep breath and let it out in two ecstatic words.

"Oh. . . . Yes!"

Eli, with the bland vague elusiveness of a man pleasantly drunk, agreed with everything and hung stubbornly to his own idea.

"Sure! Just the thing. Now you're talking. . . . Just as soon as I finish with that sonuva. . . . Just as soon as I settle a little piece of business to-morrow. Gimme one day and I'm with you."

The best he could get out of Eli was a promise to meet him there again first thing in the morning.

Eli followed him out the door, took him by the lapel of the coat.

"You see how it is, Bob, old head. No sweeter better woman never lived. . . . And that dirty sonuva . . . well I owe it to her. And I owe it to myself. If I pulled out of town now before he does, after the way I've talked around, they'd all think I was skeert."

Robert remonstrated a little but saw it was useless. The only chance was to get hold of Eli in the morning, persuade him Fowler had left town— anything to keep him sober and get him out in the hills.

When he went to the room and knocked the next morning about nine Emma opened the door to him. She was in a nervous flutter not far from hysteria.

"He left here about daylight," she told Robert. "He drank all that was left of that bottle of wine and I know he's out there getting himself all lickered up. If somebody don't stop him he'll get himself killed. You know he can't fight no more'n a baby. When he thinks he's got to fight he gets himself so drunk he don't know what he's doing. That's what he done the other time and it was only luck they didn't kill him. . . . O please go get him! Bring him back to me! Have him arrested or anything. . . . If only I could take him off some place by himself like you said . . ."

From saloon to saloon Robert went hunting his man. Eli had been in several of them, but where he was now nobody knew.

"I tried to quiet him down and shut him up in the back room there," Jim Curley told Robert. "But the goddam little idiot's got to the point now where he thinks he can lick anything. . . . And he couldn't hit a door. If he does find Fowler he's a gone goose."

Robert was crossing the nearly empty plaza, all black shadow and white sand in the morning sun, when he saw Eli coming. He recognized the bright blue suit and the great white hat, too big for the man. Eli was mounted on a fine black horse. He was coming down a side street into the plaza at a fast gallop with his big six shooter shining in his hand. The way he rolled loose and easy in his saddle showed how drunk he was. . . . In front of the open double doors of the Barney and Holt place he suddenly pulled up, throwing his horse to its haunches in a great spurt of sunlit dust. He whirled it and rode right into the door, shouting something and waving his gun. Robert started toward the place on a run as Eli disappeared. He heard a shot. Then Eli came spurring out, turned in his saddle, shot at a window that smashed, went weaving down the road in a drunken gallop.

Shots brought the plaza to sudden armed life. Men popped out of almost every door with Winchesters or six shooters in their hands. Most of them stood staring, but Arthur Barney, who came running out after Eli with a rifle, didn't hesitate a second. He raised his gun and began pumping little spurts of blue barking smoke at the wavering horseman. It was a signal for all. Four others fired almost at the same instant. Eli tossed up his arms as though in a gesture of careless assent, slumped off his horse sideways and lay curled up on the ground, looking like a dropped blue rag.

When Robert got to him, he was the center of a noisy group. Several men were kneeling beside him, turning him over, pointing out his wounds and talking all at once.

"There's where I nailed him," Arthur Barney claimed, pointing to a bullet hole behind Eli's ear. "He never knew what hit him."

"You never touched him!" answered a wide-hatted fellow with a Winchester in his hand. "I hit him first. I dusted him on both sides."

"What was he trying t'do?" asked another man as he threw an empty shell out of a shot gun. "Hold up the bank?"

"Damned if I know," said Barney. "He rode into my place and claimed somebody was hidin' there and then started to shoot. . . . Well, he got his. I nailed him the first pop."

"You never. . . . I dusted him on both sides. . . . Who the hell is he, anyway?"

"Listen here, gentlemen . . . cut the argument." It was old Amos Cartwright, the Justice of the Peace talking. "We had to shoot this fellow but we don't have to complicate the matter no more'n necessary. . . . I'm gonna hold an inquest right now and you fellers are gonna bring in a verdict that this boy met his death at the hands of parties unknown . . ."

When he had done what little there was to do Robert walked back slowly toward his hotel, feeling old, weary and small. . . . He who had been a radiant center of energy, changing the face of the earth, was suddenly shrunk to a fragment of life that could end at the pop of a gun. . . . Sorry, too, but more for Emma than for Eli. . . . He wouldn't after all have gone back to the old life and he couldn't have lived the new. . . . It was the silver that killed him.

Chapter Eight

SUNDAY was the only morning Robert lay late in bed. On this day Mrs. Latz neither served him nor bothered him. She went to church in the morning and spent the afternoon in a many-houred *kaffee klatch* with two ladies of her own nationality and generation. One week in three this gathering was held in Robert's sitting room. The first time he came home and found it there he felt that Mrs. Latz was really getting a little too high-handed, but any objections he might have made—and he had never felt sure of the courage to make any— were forestalled by Mrs. Latz bringing him on a silver tray a huge square of hot coffee-cake covered with chopped nuts, sugar and cinnamon, and a cup of strong coffee with whipped cream. He had sat in his own room, like a little boy banished from company, munching his excellent snack and reflecting upon the subtle and unforeseeable difficulties which beset all a man's dealings with women. The moment seemed to be one of a long procession of moments reaching back to a barely remembered mother. Everything a woman had ever given him —a piece of cake, a kiss or all she had—a woman gave so you couldn't refuse and refused so you

couldn't protest. A man might run from women
but if he thought he could manage them he was a
fool. This reflection made him feel old and profoundly sophisticated and took his mind entirely
off the matter at issue.

Mrs. Latz would not be in the house at all to-
day. It was one of the first things he thought after
waking and with a sense of relief.

He was so tired he felt only half alive. He looked
at the clock, incredulous, looked again. It was
nearly noon. He had slept thirteen hours after a
very hard and almost sleepless week of work, talk
and drink. He felt wearier now than when he had
when he went to bed . . . and old.

Whenever his spirits were low of late he thought
of the fact that his youth was about over. This
morning his years lay like a weight of stone on his
belly. He was conscious of them in every joint and
in the small of his back. When he yawned he felt
the lines in his face like old and hardened scars.

His past pursued him, too, as it always did at
such times, in burning twinges of remorse and regret. Things of yesterday and of years ago came
back in jumbled sudden painful images. . . . Eli.
. . . Could he have saved him? What should he
have done? No, Eli was probably doomed. . . .
That poor woman weeping on his dead shoulder.
. . . It was hell!

He thought of money he might have made,

women he might have had. . . . What had seemed
a path of glory the other night when he was drunk
now became a record of guilt and folly. His consciousness was a body that ached with old wounds
in the gray fog of his depression. He had blundered so much and wronged so many. . . . Elizabeth! . . . He always thought of her when he
was weary. She was a permanent guilt that kept
him humble. She was a stain of blood that would
not wash. . . . When that ghost got on his trail
it was time to move.

He rose wearily and went and stared in the
mirror at the touseled unshaven head that emerged
from his flannel night shirt. Old and drawn he
looked and he could see a gray hair in his sprout-
ing beard like a tiny shining blade—the first of
an army that would kill him by inches.

Shaved and dressed he sat in his front room
staring without interest at a St. Louis paper four
days old. Times he could remember when an eastern paper a month old was hot news. God, how
long ago!

Something he had to do to-day. . . . He was
aware of a duty or a purpose buried somewhere in
the deep inertia of his mind, striving painfully to
become conscious, eluding him like a known but
forgotten name. He knew nothing about it except
that he didn't want to do it. To contemplate any
effort this day was pain. But he had never spared

himself. Conscientiously he began going over all his affairs, counting them off on his fingers—the mill, the store, the mine, Tom, McMasters . . . Robinson . . . Emily . . . that was it! To-day he was going to call on Emily, take her for a drive, be invited to dinner, try again. . . .

Shamelessly he shrank from it. Not that he cared for Emily any less nor wanted any less to marry her but he didn't feel equal to the effort and tension of such a formidable social encounter. . . . Had he said Sunday or just some time soon? He couldn't remember. It would be terrible if they expected him and he didn't get there. Plausible lies went flashing through his mind . . . mudholes, hotboxes, broken axles, sudden illness, called out of town . . . any of them would do. And maybe he would feel more like it later.

He didn't make up his mind. He merely sat inert, wholly unable to lift the vast burden of plan and intention he had laid upon himself. For the moment he was sick of all the things that made up the strenuous exciting uncompleted pattern of his life—silver, lumber, railroads, real estate . . . Emily. . . . No he was not sick of Emily. She remained securely his ideal of civilization. But she also was a part of his intended achievement, a challenge to his strength. And he had no strength to-day. Just now he longed to crawl out from under all his hopes and obligations, he longed to lose himself in something sweet and easy. . . .

As always when he was tired his mind went roaming back to days when he had been soft, and pervious to vagrant feelings—a shapeless mass of impulse moulded by what it touched. Thinking back upon his days of trial and error, of shame and thrill, he realized how hard he had grown, disciplined by doing. His weary spirit chafed against the rigid form struggle had laid upon it and knew no way out. He could work and sleep but when these failed him he was empty. Once he had read books. Emerson's lectures had seemed to set him free, and Don Quixote, a hard lesson at first, had finally become a delight. . . . Once he had read books and thought long thoughts but now he worked and slept.

Always in this mood it seemed to him that if Elizabeth had lived everything would have been different. Elizabeth had been music, memory and devotion. . . .

His mind went roaming back. He thought of the cavelike coolness of little adobe saloons, of air heavy with the smell of native wine, of the tinkle of music on summer nights, of doors furtively opened and hands meeting hands in the dark. . . . A soft reminiscent sensuality, mixed with regret and longing, warmed his blood. It weakened him as though taut wires inside him had gone slack. . . .

He rose and walked about the room, impatiently, shaking off his mood like the dust of a tumble. He had been young, yes, and foolish and he didn't regret it . . . not as a whole . . . only some things. . . . But he feared this weak and useless hankering. He feared the strong hot currents of emotion that sweep a man off his chosen course. He feared them with the deep instinctive fear of the man who knows himself to be soft inside his shell.

Walking around he began to feel hungry. He had forgotten to eat, as he usually did when Mrs. Latz left him to forage, until his emptiness forced itself upon his attention. He welcomed his hunger because it broke his mood and gave him something to do.

In the spacious spotless kitchen with its great black and nickel range and its ordered ranks of bright utensils he began a fumbling noisy search for what he needed, boldly planning ham and eggs without knowing where either was to be found. While he was at work he heard light footsteps and a snatch of a song.

Annie! He had forgotten all about her, hadn't thought of her once since the other night. Moreover, he didn't want to see her now. He didn't want to see anybody. He thought of sneaking out the back door and going down town for breakfast. . . . But no. . . . He couldn't be chased out of his own house. He let these two women pull him and push him around too much as it was. . . . In a bad humor he banged tin and rattled paper.

Annie continued to manifest her existence as a singing voice and a faraway footstep for some minutes. Then she opened the door a little and showed him a timidly smiling face.

"Can I help you?" she asked.

She wore some kind of a flimsy blue shift that had no shape but what she gave it by holding it tightly about her, and her eyes had that wide expectant look he used to see in them when he came back from the store bringing candy. . . . It reminded him of old times. His bad humor dissolved in a pleasant warmth.

"You sure can," he said heartily. "Come on in, Annie!"

"I better go up and dress. I look awful."

This was the new self-conscious Annie speaking and it mildly irritated him. For one thing he could see that she had fixed her heavy brown hair most carefully. She didn't look awful. She looked pink and lovely and nobody knew it better than she.

"Come on in," he commanded. "You look fine."

"Well . . ." She came timidly, hastily fixing her wrapper with a pin.

Robert felt embarrassed and ill at ease, just as he had before. For a moment he had believed he and Annie were going to become again the easy comrades they had been before she went away, but

[219]

he found he couldn't play his part. He could neither treat her as a child nor accept her as a woman.

He could think of nothing to say and she was silent too, but apparently not embarrassed. She took the matter of breakfast completely off his hands, leaving him with nothing to do but watch her. She worked deftly, with an air of enraptured delight. She measured coffee into the pot with an inscrutable smile, like a witch brewing some mysterious and powerful potion.

When the coffee was on the fire she turned and faced him.

"Now what else do you want? Shall I make some toast? Do you want some jam? I'll go out in the pantry and see what there is. . . . Shall I?"

She stood there smiling, confronting him with her question as with a challenge, and he stared at her, silent and helpless.

He could not take his eyes off her soft young mouth. Her kiss of the other night came back to him as really as though her lips were on his now.

There was no getting away from the absurd unwelcome fact. . . . It thrust itself stubbornly into his reluctant mind. . . . What he wanted just then was to kiss Annie again.

It was an irritating embarrassing desire. It made him angry with Annie and angry with himself. . . . There was mischief, it seemed to him, in her smile, as though she had read his thought.

"What'll it be?" she demanded. "Quince or raspberry?"

He cleared his throat, pulled himself together, and spoke with unnecessary emphasis.

"Quince!" he announced savagely.

Annie threw back her head and laughed a bubbling triumphant young laugh. . . . Then she hurried into the pantry.

Her voice came out to him in a moment.

"Please come and help me! Bring a match. I can't see a thing in here."

He got matches out of a wooden box on the stove and plunged into cool darkness after her.

The pantry was a large square room without a window. Its thick adobe walls kept its temperature about the same all the year around, and it was filled with a heavy odor of peppers, onions and hams that hung from the rafters and rested on swinging shelves.

He forgot to strike a match. He went in groping, with a breathless sense of mingled expectancy and doom . . .

His groping hands found Annie and they found her as willing and expectant as though this had been an appointed tryst. Their kiss seemed as inevitable as the sunrise, but its sweetness struck upon his senses with a bewildering force. It gave him an irresistible conviction of discovery—of finding something he had long and unconsciously sought. The warmth and eagerness of her youth seemed to pour through his blood, swelling the moment with a blind intensity of life that made it immeasurable. He had forgotten desire could be so keen. . . .

They came out hand in hand, laughing, at once relieved and excited. Annie was a vivid pink and her eyes were bright as sunlight striking water, but she was not flustered. She stopped laughing and made a pretty mouth of mock distress.

"We forgot the jam!" she reminded him.

He threw back his head and laughed till he was red in the face. Forgot the jam! What could be funnier? His laugh was a shout of joy and relief.

He was grateful to Annie. First she knocked his senses into a jumble and then she saved him from his own confusion.

When the jam had been found she made him sit down. She wouldn't let him do a thing. She put a cloth on the table and laid it, made toast and boiled eggs. She seemed to work with an inspired fervor. She was like a bird feeding its young—the same swift graceful eagerness of instinctive giving. He could not keep his eyes away from the wonder of her slim quick hands, the curve of hip and breast that rippled to the rise and fall of her arm.

They ate in silence, smiling at each other. He knew what he wanted to say, but somehow it seemed impossible just then to say anything.

[222]

They had nearly finished their coffee when he noticed that Annie's eyes were beginning to darken. . . . He could see doubt and fear rising in them as plainly as clouds in a sky.

He rose and went toward her, but she was already up. She held him off.

"What's the matter, Annie? Everything's all right . . ."

"No, no, no! I didn't mean to let that happen. . . . I don't want. . . . I can't . . ."

She turned and ran, slamming the kitchen door almost in his face. He stood bewildered, listening to her fleeing footsteps, to the bang of another more distant door.

For a few minutes he walked up and down, plowing his hair with his hand. Damn women anyway and especially when they cried! He couldn't stand this. An ache of distress filled his throat and his head was confusion.

He knew clearly and well that this was a decisive moment—that now, if ever, was the time to turn away and think. But he seemed completely incapable of thought. His mind was too full of Annie to work on anything else. . . . Anger he felt at first and then a growing tenderness and pity. . . . He could not turn away. He must go to her, comfort her, explain. . . . Make everything somehow all right again. . . .

He went to Annie's room and knocked on the

[223]

door. After a moment of silence a small, muffled voice full of tears told him to come in.

Annie lay at full length on the bed, a sweetly curving blue horizon against the white of the counterpane. Her face was completely buried in hair and arms and she did not move as he entered. He went and sat down beside her, began gently stroking her hair.

"Annie. . . . It's all right . . . everything's all right . . ."

She sat up so suddenly that he almost fell off the edge of the bed. She confronted him with a face heavily flushed, eyes dark with misery and bright with tears.

"Don't say anything! Please don't say anything! Please . . ."

Her choking voice exploded into a sob and she flopped down and lay weeping.

Had a geyser spurted up through the floor he would not have felt more impotent to deal with it. If only Annie would let him talk. . . . Guilty and miserable he sat stroking her hair.

Under his hand her sobs slowed and died, giving him a warming sense of power. He bent and kissed her neck where the hair fell apart on the back of it. He kissed it several times. . . . This, he told himself, was not the way to proceed. . . . He kissed her again and she turned to meet his lips.

Once more time was lost. Neither of them knew how long it had been when steps in the hall fell like drum taps on the tense absorbing silence of their communion.

The limp and prostrate Annie jerked suddenly upright, sat with wide eyes and a finger touching a frightened mouth, looking peculiarly like a child —suddenly years younger.

"It's mother," she whispered. "What shall we do? She'll look for me . . ."

"You better fix yourself up a little," he suggested.

"Sh-sh-sh!" Annie warned.

Robert laughed.

"It's no use shushing now," he told her. "Go and fix your hair."

Annie had barely finished a hasty toilet when steps marched straight to the room and culminated in a firm knock. Robert took Annie by the hand and led her, scared and holding back, to the door.

He opened it upon Mrs. Latz, who threw back her head, placed her hands upon her hips and froze into a rigid image of outraged amazement.

They stood before her flushed and disheveled, Annie half hiding behind him, like a couple of children caught stealing sweets.

Robert had felt perfectly sure of himself a moment before. He had known from the first kiss exactly what the situation meant to him. But that

grim image of parental authority and outraged
convention seemed to wither his dignity and tangle
his tongue.

"I . . . we . . . well, we're going to get married!" he blurted.

Mrs. Latz altered pose and feature no more
than a statue, but her eyes betrayed a certain mol-
lification of the spirit.

"It's about time!" she remarked.

FOURTH PART

GAS

Chapter One

WHEN the first bicycles came to town he bought one secretly and secretly he struggled with it in the yard behind the store. It was a perilous-looking thing with an enormous wooden front wheel and a tiny rear one. He found it hard to believe that he or anyone else could ride it, but he felt that he must try. He was not going to fall behind the times if he could help it. . . . Not even Annie knew that he had met and mastered this challenge of progress until he went sailing down the street, his coat tails flying in the wind, scaring horses and passing old friends so fast they didn't recognize him. Nine miles an hour with less work than walking. . . . It was wonderful!

Still more wonderful was the horseless carriage but he was a little weary of wonders when the vogue began. When he read about it he refused to believe the thing would ever become practicable, and when he saw the first one he felt sure. It was a ridiculous little cart with an engine under its seat that sounded like a bunch of fire crackers, filled the air with a poisonous stench and shook the whole contraption almost to pieces. It gave him a good laugh. But the hard clattering laughter of the little engine drowned his voice and the noise of it soon became a chorus. There were eleven of them in town before he knew it and he often heard people boast of the fact. In spite of the noise and dust and stench and the way they scared horses, everybody was proud of them.

When J. N. Sampson, President of the First National Bank, imported the first large car the crowd that gathered to see it unloaded was equal to what a circus would draw.

Sampson's car stalled on the railroad tracks and they had to flag the limited to save it from destruction. It plowed into the rear end of a delivery wagon, split the thing wide open and almost killed the driver. It started at least one runaway every time it moved. Time and again it came home behind a team of horses followed by half the small boys in town.

He wondered how long Sampson would stand the expense and how long the town would stand the nuisance. He fully expected the fad to die out in a year or two. But each year brought more cars and better cars and also cheaper cars. He never forgot the first time he heard a Ford—that scream of metallic agony followed by a hoarse cough and a volley as of muffled shots. It was unlike any sound he had ever known. He could not think of it as a thing that would last. It seemed an accidental discord in the rhythm of his life. He had learned to love the crack of a whip, the shouted curse of teamsters, the heavy rumble of rolling wagons. He had welcomed the voice of the locomotive as the shout of a triumph he shared. But the putter and screech of the flivver never ceased to torture his ear. It was the voice of a life he could not live. It made him realize that he was old.

Everyone seemed to know that he was old before he did. He had never been seriously sick. He still was lean and had all his hair and it turned gray but slowly. He had never broken down. He had merely slowed down so that he hardly noticed the change. . . . And time went by so fast. He could remember how endless days had seemed when he was young and impatient for change. Now a day was a flash of light. Time was leaving him behind.

He was one of the old timers now—significant word. He was old man Jayson to the boys. He was an old codger that came before the railroad.

A whole generation had grown up and moved in to which the building of the railroad was a remote historical event. And to him it was the last important thing that happened. It seemed so recent and yet it belonged to such a different day. Things he had used a little while ago were already stuff for a museum—the giant wagons that rotted in the yard, the moth-eaten buffalo robes that had kept him warm in a hundred camps, the rusty guns he had carried. . . . A moment ago he had been in the dust and the thick of struggle and now he found himself unaccountably sitting half-idle among a litter of relics.

He had never gone out of business but little by little most of his business had disappeared, leaving him neither as rich as he had hoped to be nor as poor as he had feared. The store had closed its doors years ago. The town no longer had any place for store-keeping as he knew it and he despised the kind that had come to take its place. In those days a store-keeper carried a whole community on his books and ruled his territory as a monarch. Times he could remember when he and Tom could swing an election, give orders to hundreds, times of drought and Indian trouble when the life of the town depended on the flour in their warehouse, the money in their safe. Now store-keeping was a matter of being polite, trying to sell for a dime what was bought for a nickle.

The saw mill was a memory too. He had cut all the timber he could buy and reach and when he looked about for more there was none he could get. It was incredible, but almost every tree near a railroad had been cut and much of the rest had burned.

Strangest of all to an old-timer was the collapse of mining. In those days when the boom swept south from Leadville and Cripple Creek, when

prospectors punched their burros over every hill
and every man had a pocketful of mining stock and
a claim somewhere that was going to be a bonanza,
when beggars turned into millionaires at the stroke
of a pick and men went mad on sudden money—
in those days, they had all thought it was the wild
beginning of something that would grow and last.
Every mining town was the site of a future city
with the plans drawn and streets laid out and the
lots sold. Then silver prices began to drop. William
Jennings Bryan went bellowing in vain for sixteen-
to-one, made men weep with his cross of gold. . . .
Even before that Socorro was dead and the Long
Shot Mine was a bat roost. The last time he went
there the population had shrunk from thousands
to hundreds. It was a ghost town with three empty
buildings for one where people lived, its sidewalks
rotting and falling, its streets going to grass. In
those days when they had a killing almost every
week and took out a million a year in silver bars
he used to wonder if the town would ever settle
down. It had settled down like a corpse in a grave
and even so it had more life left in it than most
mining towns.

The world he had lived in was dying all around
him and it became his duty to bury the dead. He
was always going to funerals. He had stared down

at more dead faces under glass in the past few years than in all his life before. The atmosphere of funerals became a painfully familiar thing—the heavy smell of cut flowers, the whispering groups in black, the long rambling speech about the dead man's life by someone who knew nothing about it, the preacher talking about God and Heaven, the peal of sad music, the sob and snuffle of women, the long dusty ride to the cemetery, the desultory talk of perfunctory mourners, the final thud of dirt on wood. . . .

Eight times in a year he was a pall-bearer. Most of the men he helped carry to their graves were nothing to him. He was asked to bury them only because he was one of the old-timers. Their funerals bored rather than saddened him. But every time he buried a man who had played a part in his life he felt depressed and diminished. He felt as though he had planted a bit of himself.

Tom's funeral was the one that hit him hardest. It seemed to push him back into the past and it seemed to leave him there. More and more each year he had leaned back against his memories, and when they buried Tom, memories came thick and vivid. Memories seemed more solid and real than the black shadowy figures in the room, and when a young lawyer who had worked for Tom got up to praise the dead pioneer, the living one went marching through Robert's mind.

[234]

"This man has had his reward on earth as he will have it in Heaven. In the days when this land was a barren and hostile wilderness he suffered and fought and toiled and he lived to enjoy the fruit of his labor. He lived to see the desert blossom and a splendid city spring out of the soil watered by the blood of his generation . . ."

On and on in easy eloquence went the young man of many words, pitying the old-timers for their sufferings, patronizing them with unwanted praise. . . . Robert felt like getting up and telling them all the old days were not as bad as they imagined. It was no hardship to live in a time when land and gold and timber were there for the taking and a man could do as he pleased. And if this town was the fruit of Tom's labor, he had certainly found a worm in his apple. It had been his pride to own the finest bar south of Denver and to run games that were as straight as a church raffle. . . . First the women and preachers put through an anti-gambling law, and then they closed the saloons. Tom was left with money enough—he sold his corner saloon for more than the whole town was worth when he bought it—but he had no more occupation than an iceman in hell. He spent his last years raising game chickens that never fought and driving a trotting horse that was gradually crowded off the roads by the growing auto traffic. An enormous man with a bright red face and white hair, he was known by sight to everyone in town, but few knew much about him. Some wit said he looked like something prehistoric. . . . To the last he cursed reformers with a thunderous unction that recalled his mule-driving prime. Their laws were a personal insult to him, because Tom had always been a law-and-order man. In those days when he started in the liquor business, he was always saying that what they needed were churches and homes and good women. He had regarded his saloon as a monument to civilization—a place where life and money were safe and every man was a gentleman and a good sport as long as he stayed inside and when he fell from grace he landed in the street.

Tom had been a leader in the fight against the tinhorns and blacklegs that came in with the rails. He had done more than any other one man to get Diego elected sheriff the second time when the tinhorns put up a bad-man named Carruthers to beat him. . . . On that unforgotten election day every hack and buggy in town was busy hauling voters to the polls. Tom was in charge of the transportation, he gave the free liquor and he organized the gang that watched for repeaters at the voting booths. The tinhorns bought votes outright but the old timers, with the dignity of Democratic institutions in their keeping, gave only drinks and free rides. There were arguments and fist fights all day long. Then, of course, both sides claimed the election. Each of them started a parade of victory in the evening, and the two processions with their brass bands and torches met in the plaza.

That was the biggest riot the town had ever seen. Forty or fifty men fought with fists and bottles and tin kerosene torches. Mexicans were using knives and it was only a matter of time till the guns would begin to pop. It looked sure to be a slaughter.

Then came Diego on a big bay horse. With a drawn gun he made the mob scatter like sheep before a thunderstorm. . . . Robert would never forget how Diego looked that day, a perfect horseman, hatless and gun in hand, smashing a riot by the sheer force of a courage nobody could match. It made Robert feel again as he had felt when he first met Diego—an envious, unwilling admiration —a conviction of something lacking in himself.

That was Diego's big day, the high point in his whole career. After the rumpus was over he walked up to Carruthers in Tom's saloon and slapped his face. He didn't show a gun. He just slapped the man's face and dared him to draw and Carruthers didn't dare. Diego put him in the new stone jail and mounted a guard outside with Winchesters in case the tinhorns wanted to try to get him out. But they didn't try.

Diego served out his second term as sheriff and

in all that time there was never a man shot unless
Diego shot him. The town had never been so or-
derly and quiet. And then Diego was beaten, and
not by the tinhorns but by a new reform party led
by a preacher. They made all sorts of scandalous
charges against Diego. They claimed he was pock-
eting a profit on the meals he fed the prisoners in
the jail, and he couldn't refute the charge because
he kept no books. They proved easily enough that
he gave jobs to as many of his relatives as he
could. Every deputy he commissioned was at least
a third cousin. And the jail, they claimed, wouldn't
hold any Mexican who had the remotest connection with the multitudinous clan of Aragon. One
of Diego's old sheep-herders might be arrested for
drunkenness one night, but after getting a bath and
a square meal at the expense of the county he
would be out again next morning. . . . Diego also
had a way, irritating to finicky persons, of usurp-
ing the functions of the judiciary. A bad fellow
known as Squirt Ballard came to town and made
one of the last attempts in its history to shoot it
up in the good old-fashioned way. Diego, who had
known the man for years, arrested him, led him to
the city limits, and told him if he ever showed his
face there again it would be his last day on earth.
Squirt came back, got drunk and tried it again. The
next morning he was hanging from a rafter on the
porch of the jail. They tried to tell Diego the man

hadn't had a fair trial. Diego insisted that he had been treated not only with justice, but with generosity. He couldn't understand any of the charges against him. His job was to tame the town and he had done it. What the hell did they want?

When he was beaten at the polls it broke his heart. And he had been broken in fortune long before. Old man Aragon must have left him at least two hundred thousand, mostly in land and sheep. Diego was always borrowing on his property and then borrowing more to meet payments on his notes. The woman he married took away a big chunk of his estate. She was a person of mysterious origin with bright blonde hair and a figure that looked as though it had been turned on a lathe. She opened a little shop where she sold toilet articles to women. The gallant Diego was short and easy work for her. When she got ready to leave him she had no difficulty in naming corespondents, for Diego was as naturally polygamous as a buck in November. He had been raised on polygamy, beginning with the Indian slave women in his father's house. When the courts let his beautiful blonde walk away with most of his money he lost the last of his faith in civilization. For a few years he hung around the town, drinking too much, getting fat, bleary-eyed, boastful and quarrelsome. For a long time now he had lived on a little ranch which was the last bit of his heritage.

It was hardly more of a home than one of his father's peons had held in the old days—a small adobe house under some cottonwood trees, a bit of orchard and farmland, an alkaline pasture that kept alive a cow and a team of horses. There he lived with a few of his old retainers to wait on him and listen to his curses. He had grown almost deaf and seldom came to town.

And Diego was not alone in his ruin. Almost all of the old Mexican families had lost their money and land, had fallen to pieces just as their great houses had done—those huge sprawling homesteads, with walls four feet thick, built around two and sometimes three courtyards, covering often an acre of ground. There had been one of them every few miles along the valley from Taos to El Paso. With their wide lands about them, their great store-rooms full of meat and grain, their troops of servants and their prolific women, they had seemed as safe and permanent as anything man could build. But the railroad wiped them out. The Mexicans were no good at business and couldn't make money enough to keep them up. The hands of slaves had built them and kept them intact by incessant plastering. When they were deserted their mighty walls melted in the rain like sugar.

Robert had called on Diego many times to talk with him about the old days. Diego was always delighted to see him. He would clap his hands and an ancient servant would bring a plate of white cheese and honey and a pitcher of red wine. Diego still had some plates and pitchers of the hammered silver that had filled his father's house. Most of that old silver had long since disappeared. It had melted and run a bright stream into alien pockets. The sight of those old dishes and the smell of native wine always brought Robert a curiously vivid recollection of hands, voices, rooms—made long dead moments jump alive as they never would without some physical suggestion. In fact, these unchanging things carried him back to the past more effectively than Diego did, for as he grew more and more deaf Diego seemed less and less himself. The old cocky, aggressive look and the air of aristocratic self-assurance were gone. He would lean forward and cup his ear with an eager bewildered expression like a lost man striving to catch some faraway familiar sound.

It had become very hard to talk with Diego. Now that Tom was dead, who would talk with Robert about the old times? He had long been accustomed to visit Tom at his office whenever he felt lonely. They would have a drink of Tom's twenty-year-old Kentucky Bourbon and then sit like Quakers in meeting until one of them thought of something. Once they were started, memories came tumbling out in eager talk. Jokes thirty years old woke to laughter and the blood of historic tragedies was spilled again. They went farther and farther back even to days before they had met. Robert never knew about Tom's early life until they were both old. Tom had grown up on a good farm in Missouri and if you asked him why he had gone West he always said because his father used to whip him every Saturday night. Not that he minded the whippings. For years he took them as his due and he never held them against the old man. But on a certain day he took it into his head that he could whip his father and he tried it. The old man gave him an awful lacing—he told it with pride—and the next day he started West. There were no hard feelings, apparently, on either side, but the time had come for the young bull to leave the herd, and West he went as a matter of course. The old man gave him ten dollars and a new pair of shoes, his mother put him up a fine lunch and shed a few tears over him and off he went, never to return. He walked to Independence and spent only a dime on the way and that for a plug of tobacco. People took him in, fed him and sent him on. Then he got a job in the wagon trade, like a thousand other penniless boys, and worked his way to Santa Fe. After a few years of freighting he became a mule packer with troops in the Apache country. About his life among the Indians he was always a little reticent, as though he had seen a good deal a white man had no right to know. But he could talk Apache and he had seen the inside of a medicine lodge, which proved that he had been made a member of the tribe. Robert suspected that he had been a squaw man for several years and had pulled out to save himself from going wholly wild. Men did that, especially when they fell young into Indian ways. They got so they liked tepee smoke and squaws better than houses and wives. . . . Tom had never married. . . . Robert looked about curiously at the funeral to see if by any chance Grace had come. It would have been like her, for she and Tom had become cronies when they were old, drawn together by the memories they shared. . . . Grace had held her own at the old stand for more than twenty years. The business section of the town had grown up all around her brick house with its shaded red light over the door. It was a town institution. Probably half the boys that grew up there were taken down to Grace's at a certain age. Her place had the reputation of being safe and she always stood in with the police. But after they had run out the gamblers and closed the saloons, the purity campaign came along and prostitution was officially abolished. Grace retired with dignity and a comfortable fortune to a place a little way outside the city limits and there ran a roadhouse where anyone could get bad liquor and certain choice spirits could get good.

. . . Even ladies of the highest respectability now
sometimes drank her cocktails and danced to her
music, for it was fashionable to visit roadhouses.
And Grace had a certain obscure but recognized
standing as an historical landmark. She was one of
the last of the old time Madames, the organizers
of prostitution in its palmy days. They were all
women of real force and ability as they had to be
to hold their own.

Robert had driven out once with Tom to visit
her and she greeted them with a warmth that recalled the old days. "Come in, old timers! Goddam your eyes, it does me good to see you!" She
was enormously fat with two chins and beginning
to raise a third. The figure that had started fights
and ruined fortunes was literally buried in adipose.
The only things about her that seemed the same
were her voice and her hands. Her hands were still
white and shapely and still covered with heavy old-
fashioned rings. Over fine whisky Grace got from
across the Mexican border they talked for a long
time. They went clear back to the days when all
three of them used to meet at Tolliver's, when
Tom used to catch Grace and put her on his knee
and Robert was a shy young stranger sitting in a
corner. They sat silent for long moments, staring
back with a sort of tender amazement, with wist-
ful smiles, at the incredible creatures they once
had been, the strange world they had lived in.

Grace ordered another round of drinks and they took a new lease on memory and brought back to life the town that had flowered at the railhead in a ruck of shack and tent, a cloud of dust and a crash and rattle of conquering energy. Everything was forgotten now except the great expansive moments. They remembered battles, jokes and celebrations. Those days came back to them as a thunder of hearty conflict, a rhythm of dancing feet, a shout of laughter. . . .

For her present life and the customers that came to her, Grace had nothing but contempt. She was only a dignified bootlegger now. She kept no girls because the boys, as she said, all brought their skirts along. "And you can't tell what kind they are by looking at them neither." Grace longed for the good old days when a lady was a lady and a whore was a whore.

After twenty years of mutual hostility she and Tom were at one in their contempt for the new town and the new ways. Robert did not feel as they did. He had never been a severe or a confident critic of anything. He looked upon the young with a tolerant if a bewildered eye. He would have liked to take a larger part in life, but little part was left him and things he remembered fairly blotted out the things he saw.

He realized this painfully as he followed Tom on his last ride. More than ever he felt a stranger in the city he had helped to build. His mind held a permanent picture of what had been, and he looked with recurrent surprise at the strange and changing thing that was. Where he remembered prairies and rutty road were the town's nine proud miles of paved street, all lined with neat little bungalows, with lawns and small but hopeful trees, and shiny cars waiting to whizz silky women to town. . . . And the business section seemed to grow like corn in June, straight up in the air, mounting a story or two every year, until now they had an office building eleven stories high with an elevator where the old First National Bank had done business in a one story adobe. . . . It was a fine hustling town. . . . What was the matter with it? Nothing, except that it was no longer the creature of his will. It held no adventures for him. . . .

Tom's funeral made him realize that he belonged to the past but the year that Annie died was the one that really ended his active life. Annie had always been youth to him. She had always kept him in touch with things he would otherwise have missed, and he had counted upon her more and more. . . . He had counted upon her to outlive him and bury him, and it seemed unfair for her to die. He felt as though she had gone through a door and slammed it in his face as she had done so often when they quarreled. Always before he had followed and found her and they had made it up, but this time he could only sit down bewildered and wait.

It was a cancer that killed her. She was sick a long time and for months he knew she was going to die, and yet it took him months more to realize that she was dead.

Their daughter Margaret came down from Denver for the funeral and so did her husband, John Corley, whom he saw now for the first time since they ran away and got married. John shook hands with him shyly, but with an honest grip. He felt sure there were no hard feelings any more and he was glad of that. More than once he had been tempted to write John and tell him about that night, but it would have seemed disloyal to Annie.

Margaret was almost a stranger to him—a beautiful full-figured woman with an expensive voluptuous look about her even in plain black. John had made money and he had lavished it on Margaret in the form of diamonds and platinum and fur. She held herself proudly at the funeral with everybody staring at her until the end, when they started to file out of the room. Then she broke down and ran into the back hall. Robert followed her after a few minutes of hesitation. When he looked through the door he saw her sitting there alternately dabbling her eyes with a handkerchief and taking deep puffs of a cigarette. . . . She hadn't heard or seen him and he turned and went quietly back. After all, he had nothing to say to her. He hadn't had much to say to her or about her since she was little. He used to give her candy then, and play with her, just as he had with Annie, but the older she grew the more her destiny passed into Annie's hands. If their boy had lived it might have been different. He had ideas about bringing up a son but none about a daughter. He would probably have spoiled her if she had been left to him, but she was never in any danger of being spoiled by Annie. Annie was strict, and she was ambitious for the girl. When Margaret wasn't in school she was tied to the piano for hours pounding out scales and she also took drawing and dancing outside of school hours. Then she went to Los Angeles for two years to be finished and came back to make her debut.

That was where the trouble started. In the first place, none of the town boys were good enough for Margaret in Annie's opinion. She disapproved of every suitor. And she was shocked and disgusted by the manners of the younger set to which Margaret belonged. Her ideas were old-fashioned. So were Robert's, but he was a good deal more tolerant and he couldn't quite see the justice in Annie's attitude. Annie hadn't been so slow. . . .

And it was simply impossible, since automobiles had come in, to chaperone and manage the young. Wherever they went they went in cars and that made them elusive as leaves in the wind. Once Margaret called them up at one in the morning from a town fifty miles away and explained that a bunch of them had motored out there and broken down and couldn't get back for hours yet. Annie made him hire a car and go and get Margaret and when he brought her back there were words and tears. . . . There were words and tears again when Margaret came back from a party with cocktails on her breath. . . . Robert knew little in detail about this warfare between his women. Whenever it started he carefully removed himself from the possibility of becoming involved.

They gave a big dance for Margaret at the house and Robert watched it in fascinated bewilderment until he was too sleepy to see any more. It was the year of the first short skirts and it seemed to him that all of the girls had come without their gowns. He had never seen so many silken legs and naked backs and painted mouths since the boom days in Socorro and no honky-tonk had ever shown such dancing. Half the crowd was always lost in the dark outdoors. He was surprised, and at first a little indignant, but the music made his foot tap and the perfume and laughter of dancing girls threw him way back among the years. . . .

[249]

Young men came and went in their house. None of them suited Annie, but until John showed up, none of them seemed to make any impression on Margaret either. . . . John had never been to the house until Margaret asked him. These two had gone to public school together, they had known each other for fifteen years, but they were sundered by the oldest and most enduring social cleavage in the town. Old man Corley was one of the professional gamblers that came in with the railroad. He was a leader in the fight of the tinhorns for control of the town. And when he first came, he was a perfect specimen of the breed, with a poker face as hard as a rock and a record of two killings. He had dealt monte in Deadwood and Dodge and Juarez. He had played poker with Wild Bill Hickok and Bat Masters, and had pumped a Winchester in the famous battle of the water-barrels. For twenty years he had lived on the fringe of excitement that crept slowly West with the rails. He was the perfect product of hell-on-wheels. But when he saw the old game was over, he had settled down. His poker face and faro cunning had made him money in real estate and the woman he married held him to his job by handing him a new baby every few years.

Young John was the only boy, and he was a wild one. Robert had noticed that nearly all the young men of that second generation were wild.

[250]

What their fathers left them, if nothing else, was a taste for excitement. They were born trigger-fingers with nothing to shoot, born wanderers with no place to go, born gamblers with nothing better to bet on than a ball game. Young John had never held a job for a month. He got enough money out of the old man to keep him going and he went fast. He burned the streets in a little red Ford car with two bucket seats and no top. They said he had bought the parts and built it himself and that he used to take it apart and put it together again just for fun. He had rebored the cylinders and fitted it with oversize pistons and it went so fast that when it hit a rock in the road, it fairly rose and flew. He was a menace to traffic and ready to die rather than give anybody the road. . . . He was a poker player who systematically cleaned out the few who were foolish enough to face him across a table and he was a duck-hunter of the kind who would crawl into a blind before daylight and stay there till after dark. In person he was short and wide, with a slightly projecting lower jaw and a shock of stiff blond hair that stood up like a roached forelock.

In Annie's eyes he was simply a low person. Her prejudice against the gamblers was one thing her natural warmth could never melt. Her pride in the social position she had achieved by marriage had grown into her backbone.

[251]

When Margaret brought John Corley to the house the tension between the two women became too painful to last. Annie refused to leave the young people together, but sat down in the front room and practically froze John out of the house.

John was afraid of her. That was clear. And it was equally clear that he was in love with Margaret. He continued to come to the house, chiefly when Annie wasn't there. More often he drove Margaret to the gate in his ridiculous little car and left her there, refusing to come in. . . . Robert, sitting on the porch behind the honeysuckle vine, saw them say good-by one evening. Over John's shoulder he saw Margaret's face. It was a face all softness—soft curve of cheek and light of eye and soft lips parted waiting. Margaret, he knew only too well, was made of the same soft stuff that he was.

She was a miserable girl. He never knew what Annie was saying to her, but he could see that she was caught between two personalities, both stronger than herself, unable to give in wholly to either. And he could see his own unwelcome participation in the struggle coming toward him like a doom. He was not at all surprised when Annie demanded that he tell John he must not come to the house any more.

He hated to do it but he could see no way out. He felt that Margaret was more Annie's concern than his, and he agreed with her whenever he tried to think the matter out. John was no fit husband for Margaret, he had to admit. He was not the right kind of a person. But the older he grew the more averse Robert had become to meddling with anyone's destiny, especially with love affairs. . . . You could never tell how such things would work out.

His duty by Annie was clear and he did it. He told John that Annie thought Margaret was too young to marry, that she didn't want the girl to become seriously interested in anybody. . . . John saw how it was.

John did. His face turned brick red except for a whiteness about the lips. He took it as gracefully as he might have taken a punch on the nose. For a moment he couldn't say a word. Then he spoke with difficulty as he rose.

"All right!" He paused a moment. "What you say goes—about the house. It's your house and you can kick me out of it, if you want to. But about her—well, that's up to her. If she gives me the air I'll take it—see!"

He stuck out his square projecting jaw with the last word. He looked common, belligerent and indomitable. At the door he turned again. His temper broke out in an ugly rush of words.

"And don't think I want your damn dirty money either," he snapped. "I wouldn't take it. I can

[253]

make my own money!" He went out and banged the door, leaving Robert with a feeling of perfect moral defeat.

That was supposed to end the matter, but of course it didn't. Annie couldn't keep Margaret under lock and key and John had his flying flivver and a large country for his courting. Robert saw them together once, far out on the mesa, and pretended not to see.

It was about three weeks after he had sent John away that he was awakened by a rumpus out on the street in front of the house. He heard first a thump, thump, thump, which he presently identified as the sound of someone cranking an unresponsive car. After a little while it was repeated. Then he heard a man curse with deep feeling, and faintly he heard a woman's voice and what sounded like crying. He got cautiously out of bed, turned to be sure that Annie still slept, and went to a window.

It was John's flivver, no doubt of that, and he had it heavily loaded with Margaret and two suit cases. He was still cranking and still cursing and Margaret seemed to have given herself wholly to tears. "What if they come?" he could hear her say. "What if they come?"

His mind echoed her question. What if Annie waked—and she might wake any minute—what a miserable situation it would be! He never thought of trying to stop them.

"I better go back," he heard Margaret say. "I better run back . . ."

John dropped his crank and ran to his beloved. His voice fell from hoarse rage to tender pleading. He got her quiet and ran to the crank again. The Ford sputtered. "Pull down that lever!" John yelled. The Ford roared. John leapt to his seat like a fireman. The Ford screamed, shivered and vanished. . . . Robert hove a deep sigh and mopped his brow with the tail of his night shirt.

He found Annie sitting up in bed.

"What was all the fuss out there?" she demanded.

"Somebody's car got stuck," he replied with complete veracity. "They're gone now."

When the telegram came—married, happy, ask forgiveness—Annie went into a rage that lasted for days. She refused to answer. And the young people didn't come back. They went to Denver and John got a job there in a garage. He probably started as a mechanic but he was soon a salesman and before Margaret's first baby was born he was running an agency. Robert never knew just how Annie and Margaret patched it up, nor how far Annie had humbled herself, but when Margaret came to visit them with a baby on her arm and about seven-hundred dollars worth of clothes on her back, everything seemed to be all right. It seemed as though Annie and Margaret ceased to be mother and daughter then and there and became good friends with endless gossip and shopping to share. It was an immense relief to Robert.

John never came to town until Annie died. Robert guessed that this was due more to timidity than to hard feeling. John was afraid of Annie and you couldn't blame him. She was a formidable woman, one whose energy and passion were more than equal to anything she had to face. . . . How long it had taken Robert to find that out! It was strange to remember that when he married her he had felt as though he were taking over the care of a child. Noble and tender he felt and a little ashamed and still more ashamed of being ashamed! He dreaded the gossip that would come to his ears and the prospect of walking down the street with Annie and meeting Emily Robinson was one he couldn't face with any comfort. So they were married very quietly and went to Chicago on a long honeymoon.

He would never forget their first night alone in a hotel. That was their real wedding, because it was the first time their love seemed complete. Before that it had been pain for Annie—a pain that she accepted with pride and even seemed to like.

Annie was somehow either above or below all disillusionment. She had so much more vitality than imagination that she never got outside the

present moment. She forgot the past and refused
to consider any future more remote than day after
to-morrow. It took him a long time to understand
this—to realize that Annie could not share the
confusing world of hope and regret he lived in.

He was miserable about the pain he gave her,
but she seemed wholly willing to accept love as a
wound bathed in tenderness. And when she discovered that it contained ecstasy and peace she
kissed him, sighed deeply and went to sleep like
a child tired with play. . . . She went to sleep but
he was strangely wakeful and stirred. . . . That
was another one of those hours that loomed bigger than years. He lay on an elbow looking at
Annie—the white perfection of her arms and
shoulders, her childish love-tired mouth, her too-
flat nose with a sprinkle of freckles across it—and
he knew, with a thrill of something like fear, that
he loved Annie as much for her weaknesses and
imperfections as for her beauty and the pleasure
she gave him. . . . And that was something new.
. . . Elizabeth had been a dream, except for one
burning moment of pain and realization, before
she became a memory. And the soft-skinned, soft-
spoken women who had taught him love—in them
he had only discovered and embraced something
of himself, something that had been buried before.
But in Annie he was losing himself. . . . Was it
because he was older? And would he possess her

as she possessed him? At any rate, that was the night he was married. . . . That was the night he forged a bond that had held him ever since, whether it chafed or caressed him.

He thought then he was about to be rich and he gave Annie a thousand dollars to spend on clothes. It was amazing what she did with it. Whether she had good taste or not, Annie had an open eye. Certainly the clothes they bought that year in Chicago would look like monstrosities now —those enormous skirts, those corsets he helped her put on, and it took all his strength to make them meet—but they were the clothes she needed to play her part. He had never realized before how vital clothes were to a woman. Annie studied women on the street with such passionate absorption that she seemed to forget he was there and every shop window showing clothes stalled them until Annie had considered and criticized everything in it. And when she got done dressing herself she turned in and dressed him! It was then he began to realize he was not exactly going to lead Annie through life by the hand—that she, perhaps, on occasion was going to lead him by the nose. Before he knew it she had him draped in a Prince Albert and crowned with a top hat. It took four boys to carry their baggage when they got off the train at home.

Their home-coming was not as difficult as he

had feared. Everybody who met Annie seemed to like her and no man could look at her and be surprised he had married her. Some people didn't call who should have, but Annie seemed unconcerned and that all that mattered much to him.

It was the big party they gave for the Volunteer Hook and Ladder Company that established Annie's social prestige. Robert had been elected captain. It was true he had given more than anyone else for uniforms and equipment but he was honored just the same. And it was his social duty to give a party for the bunch. It could have been a stag party but Annie saw her chance. All the wives were invited and the Hook and Ladder Company was the social cream. It was far more of a social organization than anything else anyway. Whenever the fire bell rang every member grabbed his big red hat and ran to the scene, but they never knew what to do when they got there. Robert had always doubted whether he was the ideal leader for such emergencies. He couldn't shout orders with enough voice and authority. Sometimes they did put out a fire and when it was beyond them they always had a good time watching it burn. Everybody carried heavy insurance so it didn't matter much. Often a fire was more of a blessing than a catastrophe. Every time one of the old frames on Railroad Avenue burned, a better building went up in its place. Sol Rosenberg burned out three times in ten years and each time he built a better store on the ashes of the old one. He was a charter member and a strong supporter of the Hook and Ladder Company and there were those who said he wept when the Town Council bought the first fire engine. . . . It was at the Captain's Ball that the Hook and Ladder Company showed its true form. Every member wore his blue uniform and the women were all in the most formal dress they had. Two rooms were cleared for dancing, the front yard was hung with Japanese lanterns and they had three Jap caterers to serve refreshments. It was all Annie's doing and Robert was amazed at how well she did it because it was just the kind of thing he couldn't have done at all. It was a hard crowd to handle with Jews, Mexicans and Methodists, Democrats and Republicans, old-timers and new-comers all mixed up. Some of the members were strong church people and so Annie didn't serve any liquor but she had all kinds on tap in a back room and instructed Robert to prime those who needed priming and could stand it. . . . For a girl of her age she did wonders. The eyes of men followed her beautiful shoulders all the time, but she devoted herself to women, especially to women older than herself, and this struck Robert as a policy of supreme cunning. He could see she was nervous and tense as a soldier in battle but her smile never wavered until the last guest had shouted good-by from the front gate. Then she lay down on the bed and wept. . . . Robert knew they were tears of relief and triumph. He had learned something about the tears of women by that time. After he had kissed and comforted her she went to the bureau and started to take off her gown while he lay back smoking a cigar and watched her. It seemed to him as though the admiring eyes of men and the envious eyes of women had that night warmed and stung her to a new beauty, and he felt a rush of desire such as he had not known since the first . . . a stir of pride that this was his woman who tore off her gown with impatient hands and made the strings of her corset whistle as she ungirdled her conquering body for him.

For weeks after Annie died he used to wake in the morning expecting to find her still there, he used to think of her as somewhere in the house . . . then slowly bring himself back to the reality of her death. She died a hundred times in his mind, but each time the ache was less. He thought of her so often in all the different times of their life together that it came gradually to make little difference whether he imagined her as she might have been if she were still alive or as she had been twenty years ago. His mind was a procession of phantoms anyway. He lived among beloved ghosts.

He was alone now, for the first time in so many
years. After so long a journey, after touching so
many hands, he was alone again in the place where
first he had known loneliness. Like a man lost he
had traveled a long circle and came back to where
he started. . . . Some of the old-timers still came
to see him, but people now were not as real as his
thoughts and visitors hardly interrupted his solitude. He came to accept it more and more easily
for it had something natural and necessary about
it. This solitude was nothing like the loneliness of
his youth, aching with need and aspiration. He
wanted little now and he had little to give. . . .
The ministers of desire had fallen away from him
slowly, like leaves from a dying tree, and they
were hardly missed.

He was often ailing and for the first time in his
life he saw much of doctors. He consulted many
different ones because he wanted to know exactly
what was the matter with him and how long he
had to live, and they all seemed either unwilling
or unable to tell him. They all had the same manner of mysterious wisdom and hearty reassurance,
and it gave him more pain than his rheumatism
did. At last he tried a young man named Boyce
who had come West for his own health. It was
said that tuberculosis had cut him off from a bril-
liant career in the East.

Boyce was a dying man, and he knew it. He was

so lean that he looked, especially when he sat, like a skeleton in clothing, and in the bony pallor of his face only his deepset eyes, grave and unnaturally bright, seemed to have anything of life left in them. It was said that many would not have his services, in spite of his great skill, because they could not stand his silent death's-head presence.

Robert liked the young doctor, who examined him with great care before he said a word. He then told Robert calmly that his heart might kill him any time, but that if he sat still he might live several years. If he gave up cigars and whisky he would stand a little better chance, but they agreed that a toddy and a smoke were probably worth more to him now than an extra year or two on earth. After that they always had a drink and a smoke together when the doctor came, and afterwards they sat and talked—sometimes for hours when the doctor had them to spare.

This man was the first tubercular Robert had ever known well, although the care of them had become one of the town's leading industries with five sanitariums always full. He could remember the first two who ever came for their health, back in the eighties, when the new two-story hotel was built. They used to sit on the hotel porch, hawking and spitting, talking to each other and to everyone else who would listen about their symptoms, making bets as to which of them would die first.

Others took sides and laid wagers on this question. It became a sporting proposition in those days when the town never overlooked a chance to bet on anything, and the two men, shriveling in the sun, became delighted centers of interest. They were remarkably cheerful.

There was nothing cheerful about Boyce. He sometimes laughed a hard dry laughter that always ended in a deep gurgling cough, but he seldom smiled. Robert gathered that he had given up both a career and a woman to come West for his health. If he had chosen to rest he might have stayed half alive for many years, but he preferred to work while he could and then die. He was a reticent man but he made his essential confession in one sentence.

"I wouldn't mind dying," he said one day, "if I had ever lived."

Boyce was one of the few men Robert had ever encountered who would rather listen than talk. He sat so grave and silent, his face was so unrevealing, that it took Robert a long time to realize how eagerly he heard an old man's tales. Now and then he threw a curt and sudden question to turn the rambling story where he wanted it to go. He knew what he wanted and gradually Robert came to understand. . . . Boyce loved everything rich and lavish and thrilling—everything his own life had lacked. He loved tales of struggle and blood. He

wanted every detail of the battle with the Comanchees on the Little Arkansas. He wanted to
hear of long journeys, of camps where wild meat
roasted over great red fires, of prairies shaken to
dust by wild hoofs, and mountains where men had
hardly dented, the swarming abundance of the wilderness. He liked stories of the old-time Mexican
life, of the tremendous feasts they used to have,
of red wine poured from silver pitchers, of bailes
and pretty women. He wanted to know about the
roaring wide-open towns that blossomed at the
railheads and around the mines, the gaudy prostitution, the men with guns tied to their legs, the
games that ran into thousand-dollar pots.

Robert was amazed at the garrulity he devel-
oped under the prod of Boyce's eager interest. He
sat staring at visions, trying to put them into
words. Often he seemed to produce only a tangle
of language but sometimes he had the thrill of
recreating what he had known. . . . He had never
thought of his life as anything extraordinary. When
he had talked about it before, with Tom and Diego,
things had seemed commonplace that were revela-
tions to Boyce. And under the young doctor's eager questioning he discovered so much that he had
not thought about for years. Things he had longed
to forget when they happened now he loved to
recall. Memory had once been pain and now it was
a pageant.

The doctor always left him stimulated, happy. He would sit for hours after these conversations thinking of all the things he could not tell anyone. . . . What a man could tell about his life was the shell of it. The kernel was made of moments that could not be put into words.

Sitting on his porch in the dusk sometimes after the doctor had left, he felt a strange recurrence of the mood he had known first so long ago on Pawnee Rock. He had known it more faintly many times afterward, but it had not touched him now for years. It seemed as though the memories of those days, coming so vividly, brought it back again—that mood of calm unreasonable acceptance of everything, making catastrophes and triumphs look for the moment just alike, making the future a matter of the utmost unconcern. That mood of peace without reason seemed to run through the years like a core of flame, fusing those days and these into one. When it was upon him, he no longer yearned for a lost world. He no longer felt himself a stranger upon a changing earth. It was the same earth under his feet, the same murmur of life in his ear . . .

He always smoked too much and talked too much when the doctor came and often when he sat alone afterward a sharp pain stabbed at the heart that was failing him at last. He gasped for air and felt a cold warning of death all over him.

[266]

But when the rhythm of his breathing came back to him he never thought long of death. His mind went stubbornly back again to the days he had lived. He cocked his feet on the railing of the porch, relit his pipe and blew smoke at the faint cold glimmer of a star. . . . Why should a man who had lived be afraid to die?